The Case of the Unnecessary Sequel

The Case of the Unnecessary Sequel

A Doyle Malloy Mystery

Bob: Your enjoyment is totally "necessary."

Brian Landon

NORTH STAR PRESS OF ST. CLOUD, INC.
St. Cloud, Minnesota

Cover art: Jeffrey Holmes

ISBN: 0-87839-390-0
ISBN-13: 978-0-87839-390-9

First Edition, June 1, 2010

Printed in the United States of America

Published by
North Star Press of St. Cloud, Inc.
P.O. Box 451
St. Cloud, Minnesota 56302

northstarpress.com

The following story is fictional.

No celebrities were harmed in the making of this novel,

with the exception of Frances McDormand,

who received a paper cut upon reading an early draft.

Sorry, Frances.

AND . . . ACTION!

"You better gimme that bag of money, Herb, before I place a bullet right between those eyes of yours."

"You serious there, Ken?"

Ken brought his left hand up to the pistol to steady his grip. He closed one eye and aimed carefully. In the most intimidating voice he could muster, he responded, "Ya, you betcha."

In an effort to appear nervous, Herb rubbed his chin with his free hand, the one that wasn't holding the giant bag of money with a dollar sign printed neatly on the side. "Well, I'll be gosh darned," said Herb. Then he realized he had overplayed his part. Rubbing his chin had caused his fake beard to detach and tumble to the ground.

"Oops," said Herb.

"CUT!" yelled the director, Maura Coen. "Dammit, Davis—what are you doing? We can't have your beard fall off in the middle of an intense scene. It destroys any tension we've built up. And it's a waste of expensive film."

Davis Wilde, or rather Herb Gustofson as he'd be known for the next two months of filming, threw down the bag of tissue paper in a fit of anger.

"Hey, it's not my fault, okay? We have cheap costumes, cheap props, cheap . . . "

"Actors?" suggested Maura.

"Excuse me?" asked Davis. "Did you really just say that?"

"Okay, guys—let's take a break and cool down. Good work, everyone. Really," she said as she rolled her eyes.

She walked off to her trailer just outside the filming location, a small park on the outskirts of Brainerd, Minnesota. Davis turned to the actor playing Ken and asked, "Why did we sign up for this, exactly?"

Ken, or Mike Cameron as he was known to the rest of the world, sighed and said, "The payoff will be worth it."

"Are you sure?" asked Davis. "Because that woman's putting us through the ringer, and we don't even know if we'll get a paycheck out of this."

"Sure we will," said Mike. "Why wouldn't we?"

"We're getting paid a percentage of gross," said Davis. "But who knows if the film will even get released?"

"It'll get released," said Mike. "It's a sequel to one of the most successful films of all time. Everyone will want to see this."

"Aren't you a little troubled by the potential legal issues this could raise?" asked Davis. "Are you one-hundred percent certain she has her brothers' permission to make this movie?"

"She said she does, and she obviously got financing somehow."

"Sure, but not much financing. I mean, you haven't seen 'Paramount' or 'Miramax' tied to anything we're doing, have you?"

"Well," said Mike, "no."

"Exactly," said Davis. "And who's to say her brothers won't sue her and stop the film from ever getting released? Months of work, completely wasted."

"I really doubt that'll happen. The Coen Brothers don't sue people. Besides, I hear they have a pretty good sense of humor about this sort of thing."

"Are you sure they'll let this slide?" asked Davis, picking up a copy of the script from the director's chair. "This is some of the worst writing I've ever read. The characters say and do things with no clear motivation. The overuse of Minnesotan lingo is preposterous. Even the title is laughable."

"I think it's catchy," said Mike.

"'*Fargo II: Midwest Boogaloo*'? It doesn't even make sense."

"It's a metaphor," said Mike.

"For what? The boogaloo is a latin dance. Are you saying the characters are dancing back and forth with witty dialogue?"

"No, their scheming is like a dance. They keep changing partners, leading at different times . . ."

"Did you read the script?" Davis asked. "Because I really don't see how you got any of that from this piece of garbage."

"I read most of it. My lines, at any rate. It was enough."

"Your lines? Like, 'This lutefisk is making me thirsty'? I swear, Maura has seen nothing but *Seinfeld*, *Grumpy Old Men*, and *Hawaii Five-O*, and this is the result."

"You're sounding really negative," said Mike. "Maybe the movie will be bad, but at least you're acting. C'mon—we're doing what we love. Try having more fun instead of arguing with the director all day. Really, you'll be surprised how different your perspective on your job and even life will be if you just adjust your attitude a bit."

"Christ, you really are new to this, aren't you?" asked Davis.

"I've been acting all my life," said Mike, defensively. "The Guthrie Theatre's been a second home to me."

"I mean real acting, not fluffy Midwestern *Christmas Carol* nonsense. I can't believe I even took this job. I auditioned for a role on *Lost*. I could be filming in Hawaii right now."

"Brainerd's not so bad," said Mike. "Especially in the summer. It's peaceful."

"Boring is more like it," said Davis with a grunt.

Davis Wilde and Mike Cameron shared an uncomfortable moment of silence.

"At least we get to work with her," said Mike, motioning his head in the direction of a pale, beautiful brunette sitting in her assigned chair, flipping through pages of the script. Her surname was printed in block letters on the back of the chair: WONG.

"Eva Wong," said Davis. "I believe I've bumped into her before."

"We did one scene together yesterday. She's talented, that's for sure."

"Wong . . . such a funny name," said Davis.

"Why do you say that?"

"She doesn't look Chinese to you, does she?"

"She definitely doesn't sound Chinese, either," said Mike. "Her English accent took me by surprise. But she transitioned into the Minnesotan accent flawlessly. Her husband must be Chinese."

"Ex-husband, I think," said Davis.

Mike looked at Davis suspiciously. "You know her well?"

Davis shrugged. "Like I said, I've bumped into her before. In fact, I might do the same tonight."

"See?" said Mike. "Things are already looking better, aren't they?"

"Women seem to have that effect on me," said Davis. "At least, women other than our bitchy director."

"Maura's not so bad," said Mike. "Speaking of which—"

Maura Coen exited her trailer and approached the set, looking slightly more subdued than Davis and Mike had last seen her. Instead of standing near the camera with her arms folded, she sat in the director's chair and crossed her legs. She grabbed the megaphone from under her seat.

"*Okay, guys,*" she said into the megaphone. "*We're going to try this again, but we'll attempt the full scene. Tina, please affix the prosthetic on Davis' forehead. Chip, do you have the blanks loaded? Good. Everyone take your places.*"

Tina Callahan, the make-up artist, immediately went to town on Davis. She first applied a tiny sac of fake blood onto his forehead with a small amount of special glue. A string protruded from the sac which went through the prosthetic skin. She used a little more glue to fit the prosthetic skin very tightly to his natural skin. To make it look almost flawless, she applied small amounts of foundation along the edges until she was confident that Davis looked, to the unsuspecting viewer, completely normal.

"This looks amazing," she said.

"You're telling me," said Davis. Only his eyes were looking at something else entirely. Two things, to be exact.

She wrinkled her nose at him. "Keep your eyes up here, Hollywood," she said. "I'm starting to look forward to seeing you with a gunshot wound in the face. Oh, and put your beard back on."

"Whatever turns you on, little lady," he responded.

Tina made a gagging sound, then handed the end of the long string to Chip, the prop technician. He tied it tightly to the tip of the prop handgun that Mike would be using.

"Here you go," Chip said to Mike, handing him the gun. Chip had his hat backwards, covering a mess of long, curly hair. Of everyone working on the film, Chip by far looked the most casual. "Remember, the blanks will still make a loud noise. You also have to pull the gun back towards you. That'll make sure the bag of blood on Davis' noggin will burst open at the right time. If it all goes right, it's gonna look pretty freaking awesome."

Mike nodded. He took the gun in his hand.

"You ready for this?" asked Mike.

Davis grunted. "Yeah, I'm ready for it. Just don't fuck it up. I don't want to have this shit put on me twice."

"Don't worry, I won't," Mike said.

"*Are we ready people*?" yelled Maura Coen. "*Ready . . . And . . . ACTION*!"

Mike took a deep breath and began. "You better gimme that bag of money, Herb, before I place a bullet right between those eyes of yours." He pointed the gun directly at Davis.

"You serious there, Ken?" asked Davis, all traces of his true personality disappearing under a thin veil of faux-Minnesota charm.

"Ya," said Mike, taking careful aim. "You betcha."

"Well, I'll be gosh darn—"

BOOM!

Davis Wilde fell to the ground, blood trickling from a hole in his head.

"CUT!" yelled the director, although no one seemed to notice. Everyone stared, as if frozen in time.

Finally, Chip broke the silence. "That was a really full blood packet," he said.

"I don't think that—" Tina began to say.

"How'd we get it to spray out of the back of his head like that?" Chip asked.

"We—" Tina squeaked.

Mike Cameron stared at the gun in his hand. Then he looked up at the people surrounding him. To no one in particular he asked, "I pulled the string too hard?"

Then he blinked a few times and fell to the ground, unconscious.

Eva Wong, who had been sitting in her chair and watching the scene, ran to Mike and lifted his head.

"Someone call an ambulance," she yelled. When no one moved, she pointed at Chip. "YOU—call an ambulance, now!"

Chip nodded. "Okay." He pulled a cell phone out of his pocket. His hands trembled. "What do I tell them?"

"Tell them we have one man shot in the head and another passed out. Just tell them to get here!"

Chip did as he was told.

"You, make-up girl, call the police," Eva said to Tina. "Tell them the same thing."

Tina went immediately to her purse and took out her phone.

Meanwhile, as she held up Mike's head, Eva dug her own phone out of her coat pocket.

Maura Coen looked at the scene that had developed in front of her, taking it all in. She was sweating profusely. To Eva she asked, "Who are you calling?"

"An old friend," she said. "Someone who can help."

1

"What's this we're listening to?" asked Amanda from the passenger seat, a half-empty bag of Sun Chips resting on her lap. During most hours of the week she wore a police uniform, but today she was dressed casually in a pair of Lucky Brand jeans and a loose-fitting plaid shirt. "It sounds like Bruce Springsteen," she said.

"Pretty close," responded Detective Doyle Malloy, specialist in celebrity cases and until recently an officer in the Minneapolis Police Department. "This is the soundtrack to *Eddie and the Cruisers*."

"But it's not Bruce Springsteen on the soundtrack?" she asked, knowing she'd be getting far more information than she really wanted.

"No—you see, the producers of the film wanted Bruce Springsteen, but his music was either far too expensive or simply unattainable, so they got these guys instead, the Beaver Brown Band."

"You just made that name up," Amanda said. "I've never heard of them."

"Most people haven't," Doyle said. "The majority of their music only appeared on *Eddie and the Cruisers* and its sequel, *Eddie Lives*."

Amanda washed down a mouthful of chips with a swig of diet soda. "Are those movies any good?" Amanda asked. "I've never seen them."

"The first one is good. The sequel was terrible," said Doyle.

"Isn't that usually the case?" asked Amanda. "I mean, really—very few sequels live up to the originals."

"True," said Doyle. "There are some exceptions, of course. But usually they're just disappointing."

"Why is that, do you suppose?"

"Well," said Doyle. "I think it's because something is always missing. Maybe one of the actors from the first film doesn't want to do another one, so they come up with some shitty excuse as to why the character isn't around in the sequel. Or even worse, they use a completely different actor who looks nothing like the original."

"You have some pretty strong feelings about this," said Amanda.

"I've seen a lot of movies," said Doyle.

"How soon before we exit?"

"Another hour or so," said Doyle.

"Good God this is a long drive," said Amanda.

Doyle nodded. "Well, Brainerd is a long way from the Twin Cities. But don't worry, we'll be plenty busy once we're there."

"You mean working on the case, right?" Amanda asked, playfully.

"That's right, we're working on a case. I'd almost completely forgotten," said Doyle, returning the smile.

"Where's your partner in crime, sir William Wright?" asked Amanda.

"Oh, he won't be around—he moved back to England. He has a new job."

Amanda looked at him curiously.

"Just kidding—he's already in Brainerd. He sent me a text a couple hours ago. He'll be waiting for us when we get there."

"You had me worried."

"Why, you don't think I can handle this on my own?"

"Sure you can," she said. "I just like to know that there's someone watching your back."

"You should be more worried about William," said Doyle. "He's all brain and no brawn."

"Are you saying that you're the brawn of this operation?" asked Amanda. "Because if I recall, you succeeded at your last case by ramming head-first into the bad guy."

"Granted, not terribly strategic," said Doyle. "But it took a lot of strength. I basically turned myself into a human battering ram. William would have cracked like an egg."

"You're right, sweetheart. What was I thinking?"

"You better watch yourself, Officer Hutchins," said Doyle.

"Sun Chip?" she asked.

"Yes, please."

They snacked in silence a few moments before Amanda asked, "So, how much do you know about this situation?"

"Not much," admitted Doyle. "I only know the wee bit of information William's given me. We know there was an accident on the set of a new movie being filmed just outside Brainerd. Not many specifics yet, only that it's messy."

"Which movie?"

"Apparently they're calling it *First Kiss for Frances*, although that could easily be a cover-up for another movie. Major filmmakers often use false titles during filming to keep the press and paparazzi away from the film set. Makes things a little less complicated for them."

Amanda nodded.

"So how did William find out about all this?"

"He got a call from someone on the set. He's still not sure who it was from, they never left a name, only a garbled message and said it was extremely urgent. William hasn't given me all the details."

"Are you worried?" asked Amanda.

"Worried about what?" asked Doyle.

"This is your first case as a private investigator rather than a police detective. You've never really been without police support."

"I might be a little worried—after all, I have to make a living now by actually solving cases. I can't just sit in my office and pretend to be working on something and still receive a salary."

"You've had it easy for too long," said Amanda.

"Probably so," said Doyle. "Now it's time to pay the piper."

2

Doyle's road-worn Dodge Stratus approached the entrance of Nisswa Park on Brainerd's border. To his recollection, it was the first time Doyle had ever seen a public park closed off to the public except for "Authorized Personnel Only." He assumed it was the handy work of overly-protective film producers attempting to prevent any meddling with the film set. Doyle wondered what kind of fee they had to pay to close an entire park from middle-aged joggers and little kids who wanted to play on the lakeshore.

One thing Doyle noticed was yellow police tape. Lots and lots of yellow police tape, streaming across the gate, covering signs, littering the ground like confetti. Doyle thought it looked like a badly-themed outdoor prom.

"I bet we need a special license to swing on the monkeybars," said Amanda. "This place seems so secure, it's hard to believe a crime could have been committed within a ten-mile radius."

"I know what you mean," said Doyle. "I wonder how much of this was added after the crime took place, and how much was there before."

"You think all of this police stuff could have been here already?" Amanda asked.

"Sure, I've seen it happen. Sometimes the city itself is extremely involved in the production of the film. It wouldn't be surprising at all if some money exchanged hands in order to keep the police in close proximity to the film set."

"Really? Producers will just fork money over to the city council and say, 'Here ya go—make sure things go smoothly for us.' Isn't that illegal?"

"It's a rather grey area," said Doyle. "Legality becomes subjective at a certain point."

"You're definitely not a cop anymore, that's for sure," said Amanda.

A plump security guard who looked like the Michelin Man with a mustache approached from a small booth at the park entrance. He held a small clipboard that he tapped with a pencil as he eyed Doyle and Amanda suspiciously. Doyle was apprehensive when the guard neared the car, as the navy-blue security uniform he wore was so tight that Doyle feared any sudden movement from the guard could turn one of his shirt buttons into a lethal weapon.

"Park's closed to the public," mumbled the guard, as if the simple act of speaking took too much effort.

Doyle acted shocked as he looked from the "Authorized Personnel Only" sign, to the police tape, then back to the sign again.

"Why?" asked Doyle.

"Private," said the guard.

"So, no public then?"

"That's right. Back up and turn round," said the guard, spinning his hand in a circular motion.

"Actually," said Doyle. "I can't do that. You see, I'm a detective from Minneapolis. I'm working on this case. You've been doing a tremendous job keeping the public out. Kudos. Now I'm going to ask you to let me and my partner into the park so we can begin our investigation."

"Who are you?" asked the guard.

"I just said. We're detectives."

"I meant names," said the guard, as if it should have been obvious.

"I'm Detective Doyle Malloy, P.I., and this is Officer Amanda Hutchins, M.P.D."

"Hi," said Amanda. "I like your uniform."

"It's blue," said the guard.

"That's a good point," replied Amanda. She looked at Doyle as if to say, *Is this guy for real?*

"Where's your badges?" asked the guard.

As Amanda pulled hers out of her jeans pocket, Doyle said, "I don't have one. Like I said, I'm a private investigator."

"Then where's your license?"

"Well, I . . . am between licenses at the moment. My last one was damaged in the washing machine," said Doyle, not admitting that he had yet to receive his P.I. license from Hennepin County.

"That was dumb," said the guard.

"Guilty as charged," said Doyle.

The Michelin Guard perused his clipboard for a moment, then said, "You two aren't on the list. You should leave now."

Doyle was about to respond when Amanda suggested, "What if you add our names to the list?"

The guard looked at her as if she were insane. "I can't just add names to the list! That ruins the whole purpose. Stop causing trouble and get out of here."

"Okay," said Doyle. "Who's above you?"

"Jesus," said the guard.

"No, no . . . I mean, for your job," said Doyle.

"Oh," said the guard. "That's Mr. Winthrop."

"Is he your superior officer?" asked Doyle, realizing before he said it that the guard wasn't a police officer at all, he was simply a security guard-for-hire.

"Mr. Winthrop is the producer of the movie," said the guard.

"So even though this is a crime scene, they haven't asked you to do anything differently?" asked Doyle.

"Mr. Winthrop told me to not let anyone in, and if anyone gives me a hard time, I should call him," said the guard.

"So . . . " Doyle let his voice trail off.

"I guess I'll call him," said the guard.

The guard grabbed the walkie-talkie from his belt and brought it to his lips.

"Mr. W, this is Front Command, over," said the guard.

"Who is this?" came a voice emanating from the walkie-talkie, loud enough for Doyle and Amanda to hear.

"Front Command," repeated the guard.

"Steve? How many times have I told you—just say your goddamned name. I'm not playing this covert ops b.s."

Steve, the guard, took two steps backward and whispered loudly into the walkie, "Sorry, sir, but there are two suspicious persons trying to gain access to the park."

"Who are they? Teenagers? Burglars?" asked the voice.

"Worse," whispered Steve, not taking his eyes off Doyle or Amanda.

Doyle heard the voice mumble something, but couldn't quite make it out.

"Did that Winthrop person just say something about minorities?" asked Amanda.

"I couldn't tell," said Doyle.

"Who the fuck is it?" yelled the voice from the walkie.

"Two people claiming to be detectives working on the murder," said Steve.

"And . . . ?" asked the voice.

"I thought you didn't want anyone getting into—"

"For fuck's sakes, Steve—let the detectives in! Let them do whatever the hell they want!"

"Yes, sir," said Steve.

The frazzled guard approached the car.

"You may enter," said Steve, motioning for them to move through the entrance.

"Thanks, Steve. Could you tell us where we can find Mr. Winthrop?" asked Doyle.

"He has a trailer set up near the lake. You'll see several trailers there, but you'll know which one is his. It's the big one."

"You're too kind," said Amanda.

Steve furrowed his brow and said, "Move along."

"THIS IS A BIGGER PARK THAN I THOUGHT," said Amanda, as the car zigzagged along the crooked path, passing clumps of maples and elms, as well as jumbo trailers and what appeared to be a catering stand.

"I was up here once when I was a boy, and it certainly didn't look anything like this," said Doyle.

"I can't believe how many RV's there are," said Amanda. "Did everyone from Hollywood move into Brainerd?"

"So it seems."

Amanda cranked her head in all directions. "I haven't seen a film crew or even a single camera yet. I wonder where they're filming?"

"If we drive along the lakeshore and pass those trees, it opens up into another park area, which is where I'm guessing they're filming, away from the trailers."

"That makes sense," she said. "Should we try to find the producer . . . what was his name? Winthrop?"

Doyle nodded. "We should look for him soon, but I think we'll be better off finding William first. It's possible William's already interviewed Mr. Winthrop. We should catch up and make sure we're on the same page."

"Good idea," said Amanda. "Why don't you try calling him?"

At her suggestion, Doyle reached into his coat pocket for his cell phone, almost ramming his car into a cedar tree in the process.

"Should I make the call?" asked Amanda.

Doyle answered her by flipping open his phone and dialing, then making one more quick swerve.

Amanda rolled her eyes.

After twenty seconds, Doyle flipped the phone shut and said, "No answer."

"Maybe he's in the middle of an interrogation?" she asked.

"Possibly," said Doyle.

As Doyle drove along the shoreline around a large outcrop of trees, he was pleased to see that he was correct. The park opened up into a second huge area where, from the looks of the camera equipment, boom mikes, and lighting stands, the filming was taking place.

"Where is everyone?" asked Amanda. "I see a lot of movie thingamajigs and whatnots, but no people."

"I couldn't have said it better. I'm sure they've halted filming until some of the investigation has been completed. They're probably in their hotel rooms, I'm guessing."

"Hey, look over there," Amanda said, pointing straight ahead of her. "I see a couple of people in the distance there."

Doyle looked ahead. Sure enough, amongst all the equipment were two individuals tumbling about one another. "I see them," said Doyle, although he couldn't quite make out what they were doing.

"Are they . . . dancing?" asked Amanda, doubtfully.

"No, it looks more like . . . wrestling, maybe?"

"I don't think so. Too much flailing for that. Drive in closer," she said.

"Okay," said Doyle, putting some extra pressure on the gas pedal.

As they neared the couple, Doyle began suspecting he knew at least one of them.

"It's a fight," said Doyle.

"Who are they?"

As Amanda finished speaking, a camera tripod that stood between the feuding couple and Doyle's car crashed to ground with such force it sounded like a gunshot. Falling over the camera equipment was Doyle's business partner and fellow private investigator, William Wright. His hair was disheveled, his glasses crooked, and his face bright red. Doyle couldn't tell if he was flustered or embarrassed, or if he'd just been slapped around a few times.

"William!" Doyle yelled from his car, now only a few yards away. He slammed the car in park.

William looked towards the car with a dumbfounded expression. Then the confusion transitioned to pain as a slender brunette woman leaped over the now horribly wrecked tripod and landed horizontally on William, a knee making direct contact with his testicles.

William screamed, "My bullocks! My bloody bullocks!"

"Oh, shit," said Amanda. "We better separate them."

Doyle nodded and jumped out of the vehicle. He ran to William, while Amanda grabbed the mystery woman under the armpits and yanked her off William.

"Let go of me," snapped the brunette. "Get your hands off me this instant."

Doyle was intrigued that she had a British accent, same as William.

"Please don't let go of her," gasped William, holding his testicles and writhing in pain, inching along the ground like an earthworm.

"What exactly is going on here, William?" asked Doyle.

"Doyle, Amanda," said William through his gritted teeth. "I'd like to introduce you to my ex-wife, Eva."

3

This is really not necessary," said Eva, sitting in her monogrammed actor's chair with Amanda's handcuffs secured around her wrists.

"It's just to protect us all from getting hurt," said Amanda. "It seems that tempers have been flaring up here, and I don't want to take any chances."

"No, I mean I could beat the piss out of each and every one of you with or without the handcuffs. They're quite pointless," explained Eva.

"It's true," added William. "She has a ridiculous amount of martial arts training. Early in her acting career, she had some small roles in Japanese films."

"I always do my best with whatever roles I'm given," said Eva. "Even in Jackie Chan movies."

"That's great," said Doyle. "But let's delve right in and get to some answers. Why are you here?"

"I'm acting in this film," Eva said. "See the back of my chair?"

"'Wong,'" read Amanda. "You changed your name from 'Wright' to 'Wong'?"

"Not exactly," Eva said. "Eva Wong is the name I used in martial arts films. I figured I may as well keep the stage name, even if no one recognizes it. Besides, I thought it might be slightly harder for my deranged ex-husband to find me if I used a name other than 'Wright.'"

Doyle drew his attention to William. "You never tried tracking her down by her stage name?" he asked.

"I did," said William. "Several times, without success. Despite constant web research, I was always directed to promotional websites for films like *Kung-Fu Kangaroo* and *Discontent in the Orient*. I couldn't find her location."

"How long were you looking for me?" asked Eva.

"Two long years," said William. "I was about ready throw in the proverbial towel when you called me."

"You called him?" asked Doyle.

"Yes, about the accident. Murder. Whatever it was," said Eva, grimly. "Despite my strong desire to stay away from him, when I saw that unfortunate man lose the contents of his head, I knew I had to call William. Even though he has many problems, he's an extremely gifted detective."

"Thank you," said William.

Amanda cleared her throat. "It's really sweet that you two are being so complimentary to each other, but why exactly were you fighting a few minutes ago? Jeez, I thought you were going to crash into every expensive movie doohickey in this park."

William shrugged. "I suppose I can take some blame for that. Eva apparently used her actress voice to leave a somewhat cryptic message on my phone. I could hardly bring myself to believe it was actually her. But when I arrived here and saw her, well I just sort of—"

"Turned into a raving lunatic," said Eva. "This is exactly why I left him. He's a very good man, but has trouble controlling his emotions. It was the worst when he was working on all those horrible cases."

"What sort of cases?" asked Amanda.

"I was a specialist in serial murderers," said William. "It was a dark time in my life, and one I don't make a habit of discussing." William turned to Doyle. "Maybe I'll fill you in more as time goes on, but for now, let's focus on the current situation, yes?"

Doyle nodded. Doyle didn't do well around blood or bodies, and he imagined that William had intentionally withheld stories that may have grossed him out. Doyle felt appreciation for that, as well as a lingering curiosity in spite of himself.

"I still don't quite understand," said Amanda. "William, when you got here, did you attack Eva? What happened?"

"I didn't attack her," said William.

"Yes, you did," said Eva. "He put his arms around me and wouldn't stop bawling. He was like a child who dropped his ice cream cone. It was disturbing, to say the least."

William lowered his head. "I just miss you."

"He wouldn't let go of me, so I had to aim for the nuggets," she said.

"She did," said William. "Trust me when I say that our relationship used to be quite wonderful. All this bullock-smashing seems to be a new trait that I'm not well acquainted with."

"I can explain that," she said. "I was used to having a policeman with me at all times. Once I found the need to be on my own, I took some self-defense courses. They were fabulous. It was like Ball-Punching 101."

"I'm not sure we need to go much further with this," said Amanda. "William, what have you done with the investigation so far? Have you interviewed Mr. Winthrop, the producer?"

"I haven't done any investigating yet, I'm afraid," said William. "I've been pre-occupied."

"When did you get here?" asked Doyle.

"Not more than a half-hour before you," said William.

"So if you left as soon as you received the call, that would place the time of the murder approximately two and a half hours ago?" asked Amanda.

William nodded. "Yes, I believe that is correct."

"Well, we need to get started immediately, right Doyle?" Amanda suggested.

"Umm . . . right," said Doyle, realizing he was seeing a side of Amanda that he couldn't recall seeing before. She meant business. "I mean, yes indeed. Eva, you mentioned you were there when the murder took place. Can you tell us everything you witnessed?"

"I can, but I was rather engaged with the terribly-written script when everything happened. I really only saw the . . . well, the final result, I guess," she said.

"Okay, who's best able to fill us in and get us up to speed? Mr. Winthrop, maybe?"

"No, he wasn't even on set," said Eva. "I'd speak to either Chip Anderson or Tina Callahan. Chip is the fellow who does the special effects, and Tina is the make-up artist. They were both right there when it happened. You can also talk to the director, Maura Coen, but she's . . . unpleasant."

Amanda wrote the names down in a notebook. "Got it," she said.

William cleared his throat. "Pardon, but what about the gentleman who shot Davis in the forehead?"

"Mike Cameron," said Eva. "The ambulance took him to the hospital to get checked out. As soon as he realized what happened, he hit the ground like a sack of potatoes."

"I see," said William.

"We'll check him out later," said Amanda.

"By the way, Ms. Wong," said Doyle. "William mentioned on the phone to me that this film is called *First Kiss for Frances.* Is that really the title, or is it a cover-up for a different movie? I know filmmakers have the tendency of concealing the true name of a film for security purposes."

"You're a smart man, Detective. No, it's not called *First Kiss for Frances.*"

"Then what is it?" asked Doyle, his eyebrow cocked.

Eva held up her hand-cuffed wrists. "First?"

Doyle looked at Amanda and gave her the thumbs up.

"Fine," Amanda said. "But please stay under control, even if William gets under your skin."

"I'll behave, dear," said Eva.

Amanda unlocked Eva's cuffs and removed them.

Eva rubbed her wrists before reaching under her bottom and picking up her copy of the script and handing it to Doyle.

"Here it is," she said.

Doyle read the title.

"*Fargo II: Midwest Boogaloo,*" read Doyle. He looked at the faces surrounding him. "God help us all."

I didn't do it, man!" yelled Chip. "I don't kill people! I don't feel hostility towards anyone, I swear! Why are you looking at me like that? I'm innocent! For the love of God, stop torturing me with all these questions!"

Doyle coughed. "My question was, 'Your name is Daniel 'Chip' Anderson, right?' It's a simple yes or no question."

Amanda, sitting alongside Doyle in Chip's small, tidy trailer, reached out and patted Chip's knee. "Try to calm down," she said. "We're not accusing you of anything. We just want to get a clear picture of what you witnessed. That's all."

Amanda seemed to have a calming effect on Chip. He wiped the sweat off his forehead with his meaty arm. Sweat clung to his long, curly hair, causing it to clump in a not-so-attractive fashion.

"Okay," he said. "I'm fine. I'm calm. No problems here."

"Good," said Doyle. "So, you're Chip, is that correct?"

"Yes, I'm Chip," he said.

Doyle scribbled in his notebook.

"What are you writing?" asked Chip.

"Just your name," said Doyle.

"Oh," said Chip. "Okay, then."

"You seem nervous, Chip. Why is that?" asked Doyle.

"I've never seen a dead body before," said Chip.

"Never?" asked Doyle. "Not even at a funeral?"

"No, never," Chip said. "I've intentionally avoided it my entire life. It's just something I never really cared to see."

"But you're a special effects guy, right?" asked Doyle. "So I imagine this wasn't the first time you've had to make someone look like they were getting shot or stabbed or what have you."

"No, I've done that many times. It's really easy. Especially easy because it's fake. Whenever I set up an effect where someone gets blown away, I'm okay with it because the actor is still breathing afterwards. You know, except for this time."

Doyle crossed his legs. "Chip, maybe you can help us out. Officer Hutchins and myself just arrived here awhile ago, and we're not terribly clear yet as to what actually happened. Could you take us through, step by step, what took place this morning?"

Amanda added, "Please don't leave anything out, no matter how small or tedious. The smallest detail can make a big difference."

Chip nodded. "Yeah, sure. I can do that. Let's see . . . I woke up this morning, about 7:30, I think. I took a leak. I made myself a bowl of cereal. The Count Chocula was almost gone, so I actually had to mix it with some Frankenberry. It was kind of weird flavor combination, but at least the shapes were consistent—"

Amanda interrupted him. "We can move past some of these details. How about you take us to when you got on set this morning. Who was already present when you arrived?"

"Let's see here. The director, Maura. Eva, the sexy British actress. Tina, the make-up girl. She's also pretty attractive, though I hear she's nailing the producer. Oh, Mike Cameron, obviously—he held the gun. Then poor Davis . . ."

"Back up," said Doyle. "You said Tina was nailing the producer. Is that Mr. Winthrop?"

"Yeah, she's in his trailer like, all the time."

Doyle and Amanda gave each other a look of mutual interest. Doyle jotted down more notes.

"Was Mr. Winthrop on set when the incident happened?" asked Doyle.

Chip looked deep in thought, then said, "No, I didn't see him."

"So on set we have Maura, Eva, Tina, Mike, Davis, and yourself. Is that right?"

"And some other assorted crew," said Chip. "You could probably get a full list from Mr. Winthrop."

"We'll look into it," said Doyle. "So a scene was being shot this morning, I take it? What happened?"

"Well, Maura Coen—you know, she's the sister of the Coen Brothers, right? Kinda bitchy, to be honest. Anyhow, she had Mike and Davis run through a scene without any effects or anything. It was kind of a disaster. Davis' fake beard fell off, and that seemed to send Maura over the edge. There was a bit of a screaming match, and then she stormed off the set. Everyone took five, calmed down a bit. Maura came back a little more chilled out, and had us do the scene with effects."

"What were the effects, exactly?" asked Amanda.

"It was a shooting scene, so it involved a gun with what *should* have been blanks, some makeup, some fishing line, pretty easy stuff, really."

"Except it didn't go as planned," said Amanda.

"Right," said Chip. "I mean, I've done this effect many times before. People get shot a lot in movies, so I've perfected my technique. It took me a long time to register what had even happened, because it looked so damn real. I was impressed by how well I had done."

"So the bullets weren't blanks? Someone had replaced them with real bullets?" asked Amanda.

"That's the only explanation I can come up with," said Chip.

"Who actually loaded the gun?" asked Doyle.

"I did," said Chip. "I didn't realize they were real bullets. They looked just like the blanks to me. I mean, maybe if I looked closer or something, but I had no reason to think they weren't blanks."

"Who normally stores props and effects like the blanks? Who would have had access?" asked Doyle.

"Most of the props come from a prop company in the Twin Cities. They actually have a van parked out near the swingset on the east side of the park. But the blanks were part of the special effect supplies that I brought up myself. Usually whatever I use I just tack on as part of my fee. It's never been a problem."

"Where did you keep the blanks?" asked Doyle.

"Right in there, over in those storage bins," said Chip, pointing towards the corner of the trailer.

"Do you keep your trailer locked?" asked Amanda.

"No, I've never really needed to, although I think I may start."

"Probably a good idea," said Doyle. "Where are the rest of the blanks?"

"Oh, the local police already took those," said Chip. "They said they wanted to analyze them, but I'm not sure what they'll come up with."

"They'll be either real bullets or blanks, right?" said Amanda.

"Sure," said Chip. "But I'm not sure these guys could tell the difference. They don't seem very bright."

"You couldn't tell the difference," said Doyle.

"I know that," said Chip, his face reddening. "But it's not like I'm a frickin' bulletologist or something. I only have blanks, so I assume the ones I'm using are blanks. Someone had to have broken in here and replaced them with real ones."

"Well, that really wouldn't be a break-in, would it?" asked Doyle. "If you didn't lock the door, they really just had to walk in and do it. Could you have made it any easier for the killer?"

"Fuck, man—don't put this all on me! I'm sure whoever wanted Davis dead, they could have done it a ton of different ways. This movie is a suspense thriller, so there's plenty of fake weapons that could have been replaced with real ones. Or if they really meant business, they could have just walked up and shot him. It's not like my blanks are to blame for all of this. Someone used me and my supplies to kill a famous actor. That sucks, man."

"It's all right, calm down," said Amanda. "We're not blaming you for everything. We're just trying to get at the heart of what happened here."

"You've given us a lot of good information, Chip," said Doyle. "Is there anything else you can think of—anything else at all—that could potentially help us?"

Chip sat still for a moment, looking down at his folded hands. Then he suddenly raised his head. "That British chick. Eva Wong."

"What about her?" asked Doyle.

"When Davis was shot in the head, she ran over to the body and started directing everyone what to do. She didn't seem the slightest bit disturbed that there was a dead man lying on the ground in front of her, blood pouring all over the place."

Doyle felt a sudden rise of nausea just thinking about it.

"You thought that was unusual?" asked Amanda.

"Everyone else on the set was paralyzed. No one made a sound. She was the only one that seemed unaffected by what happened. It just sat with me the wrong way. She's pretty hot, though—even if she ends up being a crazy murderer. The fact that she might've been in my trailer is kinda sexy. Scary, too—but also sexy."

Doyle gave Amanda an uncomfortable look. He hadn't realized until that moment that they'd have to consider William's former wife a suspect in the murder. Doyle didn't think William would be so thrilled by that. As much as William and Eva had been fighting, Doyle could see that William was still endlessly infatuated with her.

"We'll let you know if we have further questions," said Doyle.

"Sure thing," said Chip. "I'll be right here in this trailer. Just make sure to knock—I'm gonna lock up, I think."

"Good idea," said Doyle.

5

I didn't . . . you know, screw him, if that's what you're thinking."

"Excuse me?" asked Doyle. "What are you talking about?"

"Mr. Winthrop. I didn't have sex with him," said Tina, arms crossed.

"Why would we want to know that, exactly?" asked Doyle.

"Because you guys are working on this . . . thing that happened to Davis, and—"

"You mean when he got shot in the face?" asked Amanda. This surprised even Doyle, though he could see that Amanda was trying to get a reaction out of the make-up artist.

Doyle had to admit, Tina was quite beautiful, although she clearly used far too much make-up on herself.

Tina looked down, solemn. "Yeah, that's what I was referring to. Anyway, I know you'll be asking everyone a lot of questions, and someone is bound to say that I spend a lot of time in Mr. Winthrop's trailer, which is true. But it's not what it sounds like, and before you start jumping to a lot of conclusions, I assure you it's in no way connected to what happened to Davis."

"So you're just trying to be proactive and clear the air, is that right?" asked Amanda.

"Yeah," said Tina. "I didn't do anything wrong. I'm an open book."

"If you weren't being intimate with Mr. Winthrop, but you were in his trailer with him all the time, what were you two doing together?" asked Amanda.

"I don't see how that's any of your business," said Tina, staring right in Amanda's eyes.

"For an open book, you're intentionally trying to be difficult to read," said Amanda.

"It's like, we want J.K. Rowling," said Doyle. "But you're giving us nothing but David Foster Wallace. Understand?"

"I don't follow," said Tina.

"Listen, we need every detail here, even if it's embarrassing. If you two were doing something secretive together, it raises suspicions, and you don't want to be raising suspicions during a murder investigation."

Tina, looking deflated, said, "I knew I'd end up telling you guys sooner or later. Nothing interesting ever stays secret, especially not in this line of work."

"Well, let's hear it," said Doyle with a pen in his hand, prepared to take down juicy gossip.

"Mr. Winthrop pays me a little extra money on the side to put make-up on him," Tina said.

"He's not in the movie, is he?" asked Doyle.

"No," said Tina. "He's not."

"He's a transvestite?" asked Doyle. "Is he also a homosexual?"

"Not necessarily," said Tina. "I mean, he's such a private person—I honestly can't see him being with anyone. I think, maybe, he just likes to look pretty."

"I see," said Doyle. "And you don't think he's gay?"

"I've put make-up on many, many men, Detective. They all like it, at least to some degree, regardless of their sexuality. I'm not saying he's not gay. I'm just saying you shouldn't jump to conclusions."

"Fair enough," said Doyle. "But, did he at any point compliment your breast size, or perhaps the shape of your ass?"

"Doyle!" said Amanda, punching him in the shoulder.

"Ow, hey—watch it. It was a fair question," he said.

"No," said Tina, with an expression of disdain. "But be sure to let me know if he compliments your penis size."

"Will do," said Doyle.

"Okay," said Amanda. "So you're not having sex with Mr. Winthrop. You apply make-up on him for extra cash, and he may or may not be a homosexual. While this all makes excellent gossip, I don't think it helps our investigation one bit."

"It could be relevant at some point," said Doyle.

Tina nodded.

"Tina, do you mind answering some direct questions regarding what you witnessed this morning?" asked Amanda.

"Am I considered a suspect?" she asked.

"Technically, everyone is—at least until we get a grasp of what happened," said Amanda. "Although you've already been questioned by the police. Did they give you any indication?"

"None, but they can be awfully hard to read," said Tina.

"Are they remarkably clever, like Sherlock Holmes?" asked Doyle.

"Quite the opposite," said Tina. "They asked me a couple questions. I explained that I just put make-up on the actors, and that seemed to settle it. It didn't seem like a woman being capable of murder was within their mental grasp."

"You realize we're from Minneapolis," said Amanda. "And, therefore, far more suspicious of everyone. Including you. Our questions may not be so simple."

"Okay, well, sure—I'll give you whatever information you want, as long as it keeps my name clear."

Doyle cocked his eyebrow. "Don't you want to know who killed Davis?"

Tina shrugged. "Eh."

Doyle and Amanda exchanged worried glances.

Amanda asked the obvious question. "So, you're not at all curious who switched out the blanks with real bullets?"

"I don't mean to sound cruel or uncompassionate, but Davis was a jerk. I mean, a real creep. Egotistical, chauvinistic, elitist, sarcastic. Kind of like Detective Malloy, except without the self-deprecating sense of humor."

"I'm not that bad—" Doyle began to say.

"I'm really not surprised someone finally put an end to him. And believe me, I'm not the only one who thinks this way. I didn't do it—but I assure you there's no shortage of women, probably men too, who would love to take credit for it."

"Do you have any suspicions as to who may have actually committed the crime?" asked Doyle.

Without hesitating, Tina said, "Eva Wong. After Davis was shot, she was on him within seconds. She didn't show the slightest bit of emotion. I mean, she's British and everything, but it still seemed weird."

Doyle was getting an uneasy feeling about William's wife repeatedly coming up as a prime suspect. Doyle wasn't sure what he was more worried about: William's potential reactions at finding out his ex-wife is a suspect, or the possibility that William's ex-wife was, in fact, the murderer. Doyle gulped.

"Tina, what do you think—" Amanda was about to ask a question when the conversation was interrupted by the sound of a megaphone.

"*Attention, all cast and crew. Please report to the set for a special announcement. Again, all cast and crew—please report to the set. Thank you.*"

"I should go," said Tina.

"That's fine," said Amanda. "Can we contact you later, should we have further questions?"

"Yeah, of course," she said. "I'm not a suspect any more, am I?"

"I'm afraid so," said Doyle. "Once we find out who the murderer is, then you're off the hook."

Tina looked from Doyle to Amanda then back to Doyle.

"I'm not gonna hold my breath," said Tina.

"Thanks for the vote of confidence," said Doyle.

"Anytime. Good luck."

6

Doyle and Amanda joined Tina, Chip, Maura, and the rest of the cast and crew who all formed a semi-circle around a well-dressed man with a megaphone. Cameras and boom mikes were nearby. They were only a few yards from where Wilde had met his maker.

"Where's William and Eva?" whispered Doyle, trying to not be overheard by the actors and crew.

"Maybe they went somewhere private," said Amanda.

"No way," said Doyle. "They were just fighting, why would they be getting naked already?"

"I meant to talk, not *that*. It's amazing how your mind works sometimes."

"Thanks, sweetie pumpkin," said Doyle.

"That wasn't a compliment," said Amanda.

"Anyhoo, is that Mr. Winthrop?"

"It must be," said Amanda. "See how thick his eyelashes are? That's not natural. He's wearing mascara."

"Huh," said Doyle. "I'll be damned."

The well-dressed man set down the megaphone, folded his hands in front of him, and said, "Thank you everyone for coming so quickly for this little announcement. As you know, tragedy struck our fine film production this morning. Celebrated, award-winning actor Davis Wilde, who certainly became a friend to us all, died suddenly and unexpectedly. While the police continue their investigation, they have asked us to temporarily shut down production. We do not yet know if this will be a matter of days or a matter of weeks, but rest assured we will be up and running again as soon as possible. In the mean time, the police have requested that everyone remain here. If you're staying in a trailer or RV during filming, please stay. If you've been taking up residence at a local motel during filming, please continue to do so until further notification. And, of course, please comply with all requests from the police.

"If you have not yet done so, please provide me with your contact information so that the authorities can get hold of you when needed. Feel free to take the rest of the evening off and we'll meet back here at nine o'clock tomorrow morning for updates. Thank you. Have a good night."

The crew grumbled as they dispersed.

The well-dressed man turned his back and began to walk away when Doyle yelled, "Mr. Winthrop!"

The man turned around. "Do I know you?"

"Mr. Winthrop, my name is Doyle Malloy, P.I., and this is Officer Amanda Hutchins, M.P.D. We have another partner, William, who's umm . . . in the lab right now. We're working on your murder investigation."

"You are?" asked the producer. "I don't recall hiring a private detective, let alone three for that matter."

"*Technically* you haven't," said Amanda. "But it would really be preposterous of you not to hire us."

"Oh, and why is that?" he asked.

"Because you want to get filming as fast as possible, and you can't as long as a police investigation is underway," she explained.

"But the police are already working on it! Why would I bother spending my own money on all this nonsense when the police will do it for free?"

"Frankly," said Doyle. "You get what you pay for. Have you talked to the chuckleheads who call themselves cops around here? The investigation could take months, and even then there's no guarantee they'll get the right man."

"Or woman," said Amanda. "That Tina seemed a little odd."

"Tina is fine, I assure you," said Winthrop. "Listen, how much will this cost me and how fast can you apprehend the criminal? Justice is, of course, my foremost concern."

"Of course," said Doyle, sensing sarcasm and returning in-kind. "We'll drop off the contract this evening, and hopefully have this wrapped up within a couple days."

"Really? That fast?" asked Winthrop.

"We already have a few leads," explained Doyle. "We'll go through the alibis and the clues. Although, if the perpetrator ends up killing again and again, that often helps weed out the suspects."

"Could that happen? Is there a serial killer out there?" asked Mr. Winthrop, looking visibly panicked. He wiped his forehead with a pocket handkerchief. "I'm really not prepared for all this. As a producer, you have to plan for the unexpected—but this, this is a little too much. Is it too dangerous for me here? Should I leave? Oh, I certainly don't want to die."

"You'll be fine. Most serial killers reside in Wisconsin, not Minnesota. This is most likely a one-off killer," said Doyle.

"You think so?"

"Well, nothing's for sure," said Doyle. "The entire cast and crew could be butchered before morning. It's too hard to tell at this point."

Winthrop whimpered.

Doyle slapped Winthrop on the shoulder. "I wouldn't let it worry ya. We'll take care of it. So we got a deal?"

Winthrop nodded. "Please . . . just find whoever did . . . you know."

"We will," said Amanda.

AS DOYLE AND AMANDA WALKED back to the car, Amanda asked, "What was with all the frightening mass-murdering butcher talk all about? That sort of discussion usually makes you nauseous."

"It does," said Doyle. "But I was trying to get a read on Mr. Winthrop. He seemed genuinely concerned when I suggested someone else could be murdered."

"So he assumes himself to be a target, right?" asked Amanda.

"Exactly. I didn't so much get the impression that he was concerned for the people around him, but I think he was definitely concerned for himself. I think we can exclude him as a likely suspect at this point," said Doyle.

"But we can't disregard him entirely. Remember, he's around actors all the time. He may have picked up a few tricks."

"Good point," said Doyle. "At any rate, at least he hired us. I'm glad we're actually getting a paycheck out of this."

"That's true," said Amanda. "You might be able to afford to take me out to a nice dinner."

"Maybe you're right," said Doyle. "Speaking of romance, let's go find a hotel, shall we?"

7

In Rafferty's Pizzeria, William and Eva sat across from each other in silence. A teenage busboy was kind enough to get William a plastic doggybag full of ice for his swollen testicles.

"I'm very sorry about that . . . happenstance," said Eva. "When you first saw me, you turned into a bit of a looney."

"I realize that, but honestly, can you just aim for the face next time? I'd greatly prefer that."

"We'll see," said Eva. "Is this really the best place for us to talk?"

"I checked all of Brainerd's surrounding cities—Nisswa, Baxter, you name it. This was the classiest restaurant I could find," said William.

"Not that we need a romantic restaurant under the circumstances," said Eva. "But I assumed you'd want to take me someplace more private where no one else can hear us."

"You don't mean . . . ?"

"You do want to question me about the murder, right?" asked Eva. "After all, I'm the one who called you about it."

"Yes, of course," said William. "Sorry, for a moment there I thought you were speaking of something else."

"Good Lord, even with a couple of battered tangerines in your underpants, your mind still goes there."

"Force of habit, I guess," said William. "Anyways, shall we get started?"

"Absolutely," said Eva.

William took out his notepad and readied a pen.

"Why did you leave me?"

Eva nearly spat out her Sprite. "Excuse me, but I thought we were discussing the murder, not our relationship."

"I just want to know. Once we get this out of the way, we can proceed with the murder investigation."

"Fine, fine—but how can you possibly not already know why I left? Haven't you thought about it?" Eva looked at William quizzically.

"Was I not good enough?" asked William. "Is that it? Were you looking for someone better?"

"William, for Godssake, you were wonderful . . . for the first couple years. Then you starting working more, got that so-called 'promotion.' Then you were working on those awful cases—"

"What does that have to do with us?" asked William.

"You became an alcoholic, you were never home, and when you were home you didn't show the slightest bit of interest in me. That's why I left."

"I see," said William. "Be honest, it was because I grew a beard, wasn't it?"

Eva raised her eyebrow. "You've changed some, I'll admit that. You've been cracking jokes. That partner of yours must be rubbing off on you."

"Doyle? He's an odd sort of character, but he does have some natural detective instincts. Sometimes instincts are more important than any sort of developed skill."

"And he's funny," said Eva. "Maybe he's better for you than I am."

"I don't find him very attractive, however," said William.

Eva laughed. "That's good to know. And you didn't order a wine or beer with your pizza. Why is that?"

William took a sip of his Diet Coke. "Watching my caloric intake," he said. "Actually, I haven't taken a sip since Doyle hired me. Initially it was because I wanted Doyle to think he'd hired Sherlock Holmes, not a washed-up drunk ex-cop. Then I realized how much of genuine thrill I got out of following the chain of clues all the way to the murderer. I hadn't felt that way in a long time."

"That's good," said Eva.

"When you get involved with these sort of cases, it's easy to drown in the gruesomeness of it all. I don't think I'm going to let that happen anymore. As long as I catch these people before they do it again, then I've saved lives. I think I can rest easy keeping that in mind."

"Well, I take it back then. I'm sorry I kicked you in the balls."

"No, it's quite all right," said William. "I'm sure I had it coming."

Their laughter was interrupted by a plump woman in a red uniform serving William and Eva their sixteen-inch Rafferty's Special.

After the woman left, Eva held up a tiny anchovy and said, "These people up here are obsessed with fish. On a pizza . . . can you believe it?"

"At least it's not on a wall and singing," said William.

"True," said Eva.

They both took a slice and attempted a bite.

"I think I'm going to take the little fishies off," said Eva.

"That sounds like a good plan," said William

As they plucked the anchovies from the pizza, William said, "I imagine I should start asking you some real questions. About the case."

"Yes, of course," said Eva. "Ask away."

"On the car ride over here, you mentioned something about blanks being replaced with real bullets, is that right?"

"Exactly. The effects fellow, I'm not sure what his real name is, but everyone calls him 'Chip,' he handed the gun to Mike Cameron. He's a local actor. Davis Wilde, the guy who was shot, was from Hollywood."

"How did Chip appear after Wilde was shot? Did he seem shocked?"

"It didn't even seem like he realized what had happened," said Eva. "Then again, everyone was in shock."

"Was anyone not in shock?"

Eva thought about it. "No, everyone was frozen in place."

"Who else was on set?"

"The director, Maura Coen. She's pretty bitchy—I wouldn't be surprised if she switched the bullets just because she woke up on the wrong side of the bed."

William wrote the name down. "Who else?"

"Tina Callahan, the make-up artist. I heard she's boinking the producer, Mr. Winthrop."

William wrote both names down. "Could be something there. Okay, who else?"

"Various cast and crew . . . I'm not sure. Frankly, I didn't get a chance to meet all that many of them. We didn't begin filming until just a few days ago."

"Did anything happen out of the ordinary today, or did anyone behave in a manner that was unusual?"

"I'm not sure. We were all in a foul mood, but I think everyone had their own reasons for that. Mr. Winthrop seemed particularly on edge this morning, I assume because the rumor was spreading about his afternoon romps with Tina. He wasn't on set, though, when Wilde was murdered."

"Do you think Winthrop, or anyone for that matter, would have reason to murder Wilde?"

"I think anyone who'd ever had a conversation with him would have good reason to murder to him. I hate to speak ill of the dead, but Wilde was a complete asshole. I mean, one-hundred percent skum, to the very core. He looked good on screen, though. I'll give him that."

William nodded. "Fascinating. Listen, I think I should go."

"Why?" asked Eva. "Don't you want to keep talking? After all, we have months to catch up on."

"I appreciate that, dear," William said, then stopped himself. "Er, Eva. But I have work to do. A murderer is on the loose. We can catch up afterwards."

Eva grimaced. "I guess some things don't change."

William threw cash on the table to cover the bill. "No, I wouldn't say that. I think I realize now that everything changes. It's how we cope with change that really matters. I didn't cope so well before. I think I understand myself a little better now."

William lifted the bag of melting ice off his lap and dropped it on the table.

"Hopefully they'll clear the table before this spills," he said. "Please keep your phone on in case I have more questions for you."

"Where are you going?" asked Eva.

"Out to my car," said William. "I need my laptop. I have some research to do."

"Good luck getting a signal," said Eva. "Besides, I need a ride back to my trailer."

William rubbed his chin. "Oh, right," he said. "Dammit."

"Just bring me back to the campgrounds, and you can get a connection there. They have lots of equipment set up for that, so you should have no problem getting a signal."

"I can get a signal at the hotel. Here's some cash for a taxi. I'm sorry, but I cannot be distracted right now."

Eva shoved William's hand away. "I have plenty of money. Besides, I thought maybe you wanted to patch things up. I can see that I was wrong."

William stood up. "We'll talk later, Eva. Right now, I have work to do."

"If there's a murderer at large, in the very campgrounds where I'm staying no less. Shouldn't you protect me?" asked Eva.

William looked from his crotch to the bag of ice on the table. "You know how to protect yourself. Have a good night, Eva."

Doyle adjusted the showerhead.

"Is that better?" he asked.

"Much," said Amanda. "You're an unusual man, Mr. Malloy. Most guys prefer the bedroom, especially for the first night. You head straight to the shower."

"There's too much pressure in the bedroom," said Doyle, turning the water dial to a warmer temperature. "I didn't want our first night together to be a bunch of fumbling around, trying to impress each other. In the shower, it's all out in the open."

Amanda looked down. "You can say that again."

"See, isn't this more fun?" asked Doyle, embracing her, pulling her closer.

Doyle went in for a kiss, and it was everything he hoped it would be. Passionate, tender, absolute bliss. He could feel himself really falling for her.

Amanda broke off the kiss to ask, "What is that?"

"Just the ol' dingly dangly," said Doyle, going back in for another kiss.

"No, not that," she said, pushing him away. "Did you hear something?"

Doyle listened, then he heard it, too. "Is someone knocking?"

Then they both heard a bang that sounded like a gunshot, followed by a loud slamming sound.

Doyle and Amanda jumped, then gripped each other tighter.

Suddenly the bathroom door burst open. "Doyle, are you in there?" they heard a familiar English-accented voice say.

Doyle moved the shower curtain aside so only his face was exposed.

"William!?" said Doyle, not knowing what else to say.

"Doyle, are you okay?"

"Yes, I'm fine. Just . . . taking a shower."

"Oh, I see . . . I didn't . . ." Then William noticed the lacy undergarments lying on the bathroom floor.

"You're not cross-dressing, are you?"

Amanda moved the shower curtain aside so William could see her face.

"Hi, William," she said.

"Well, this is dreadfully embarrassing," said William. "Sorry, I thought perhaps you were in danger, and I may know who the killer is, and well, I, umm . . ."

"William, go wait out in the bedroom. Turn on the TV or something," said Amanda.

"Yes, right. Okay," said William, closing the bathroom door behind him.

Amanda looked at Doyle's disappointed face. "We'll continue this later."

Doyle sighed. "Promise?"

"I promise."

"Can I kill William?" asked Doyle.

"Maybe," said Amanda. "Let's think on that one."

"THAT WAS TRAUMATIZING," SAID WILLIAM, sitting on the edge of the queen-size bed in the small, bare motel room. "I'm truly sorry. I had no idea you were in the middle of, em . . ."

"Amanda, you mean?" asked Doyle.

"No, well yes, I meant . . . in the middle of doing *that*."

Amanda walked out of the bathroom with a towel wrapped around her body. "Are you calling me a *that*?" she asked.

"No, no, I didn't mean that," said William.

"Don't worry, William. I'm just trying to make you feel terrible about interrupting us," she said.

"Mission accomplished," William said.

"I can't believe you shot the doorlock," said Doyle, admiring William's handywork. "That's some serious *Dirty Harry* action."

"I was in a hurry," said William. "I was worried about you."

"Why were you so worried?" asked Amanda, carrying a pile of fresh clothing into the bathroom.

"A killer is on the loose, and I'm afraid he or she may not be done quite yet. And, honestly, I wasn't sure how prepared either of you were."

"No need to worry, William," Amanda yelled from behind the bathroom door. "I'm capable of protecting Doyle and myself."

"Hey, I'm capable of—" Doyle began to say until William cut him off.

"You say that now, Amanda," said William. "But, meanwhile, your gun is resting on your bureau. Had I been the killer, you would have been naked and helpless."

Doyle sighed and thought dreamily of Amanda.

"Doyle, where's your gun?" asked William.

"Well, you see, I umm . . . " Doyle began to say, attempting to best to conjure up an excuse within very little time. "I, uhh . . . I forgot it at home. Sorry."

William simply shook his head.

Amanda came out of the bathroom and shrugged, unsurprised.

"Don't worry," she said. "Unlike William, I think this is a one-off kill. If the rumors are correct, Davis Wilde was not the most pleasant person. I think he rubbed someone the wrong way and maybe got what was coming to him. Whoever did it, I doubt we'll be in any imminent danger from them. Even if we were, that won't stop us from catching the person."

"Speak for yourself," said Doyle. "I have an automatic starter for my car right here in my pocket. The slightest hint of danger, and I disappear within a matter of seconds."

"My hero," said Amanda.

"But seriously, William—why were you so concerned? Do you suspect someone in particular? Do you think they're going to come after us?" asked Doyle.

"The hell of it is," said William, "I've been so preoccupied with Eva being here that I have hardly looked into the case. I only know the few things that Eva told me. I'm not usually this negligent, which frankly made me fear the worst about what could be happening to the two of you, my closest friends, while my back was turned."

Doyle looked to Amanda, wondering if she was also shocked at being one of William's closest friends.

"So, if you had to place a bet on who the killer was, who would you put your money on?" asked Doyle.

"My gut tells me it's the director, Maura Coen. Eva tells me she's a horrible person, and that most people feel the same way. Tina, the make-up artist or Winthrop, the producer, are both intriguing suspects. I understand that they've been intimate, which means this could be a classic example of a love-triangle gone wrong."

"Tina and Mr. Winthrop haven't been intimate," said Amanda. "She told us right off the bat that Winthrop pays her extra money on the side to apply make-up on him in the evenings."

"Hmm, fascinating," said William. "Of course, just because she said that doesn't make it the truth."

"Yes, William—people can lie. Do you suspect anyone else?" asked Amanda.

"Not at this point. Not without further investigation," said William.

"You know, some of the cast and crew suspect someone else," said Amanda.

Doyle looked at Amanda, knowing where she was going with the conversation. He shook his head, trying to cut her off.

"Who? You don't mean . . . " William said, his face frozen for a couple moments before a hearty laughter overtook him.

Doyle sighed with relief. He had feared an angry explosion from William if his Eva were implicated, and was pleasantly surprised when it didn't happen.

"Listen, I've known Eva for years. She can be rough around the edges, yes, but she's not a killer. I can assure you of that."

"Maybe," said Amanda. "But she's still a suspect, just like everyone else who was on set early this morning."

William nodded. "You're absolutely right. I certainly won't disregard anyone. But Eva . . ." William said, holding back another snicker. "Oh, you two make me laugh."

Doyle and Amanda looked at each other uneasily.

"Listen," said William, suddenly standing. "Why don't you two get dressed, ready, what have you, and let's get going."

"Get going?" said Amanda. "It's after 10:00. It's night. We can continue tomorrow."

"No, no—we can't wait. The longer we wait, the more of an opportunity the killer has. We need to start with the basics. Have either of you seen the body yet?"

Doyle and Amanda shook their heads.

"Okay, then. First stop, the morgue. After that, let's go back to the scene of the crime. See if we can find any clues. Anything the cops missed. Based on what I've seen so far, they may have missed quite a bit."

"Then what?" said Doyle.

"Then, after two to three hours of sleep, we talk with the lead investigators, let them know how much they've tainted the process already. And then take over," said William.

"That's somewhat presumptuous, isn't it?" asked Doyle.

"That's a big word for you," said Amanda.

Doyle shrugged. "It was on my 'word-a-day' calendar yesterday. But you see what I'm getting at, right? These local cops—sure they seem a bit . . . em . . . 'rural,' but that doesn't mean they're not talented detectives. Who knows, they might already have this thing all figured out. Besides, they're certainly not going to let a few PIs take over a major investigation, especially one that will attract a lot of news attention."

"We'll see," said William. "Now get ready. We have work to do! I'll wait in my car."

He was about to walk out the door when he pointed to the disfigured doorhandle, turned his head, and said, "Doyle—you might want to explain this to management, or else they're not going to be very happy with you."

"Thanks for the advice," said Doyle.

Really, what's the point of coming here?" asked Doyle.

"That's what *he* said," said Amanda.

Doyle looked aghast at Amanda, then gave her a high-five. "Nice," he said.

"Thanks," said Amanda.

They stood outside the doorway to the Nisswa morgue, which was actually a small room inside the Nisswa Municipal Hospital. The morgue was located in the rear of the building so people driving by wouldn't know it was there. Dead bodies weren't something one usually liked to associate with small town living.

"But seriously, why are we at the morgue?" asked Doyle. "We know he was shot in the head. It's not like the last case where we didn't know if it was an overdose or murder. I think this one's pretty self-explanatory."

"That may be true, but you never know what evidence you might find," said William. "Without a thorough examination, we won't have all the evidence. Even if we find nothing, at least we'll have covered all our bases."

"Fine," said Doyle. "But I'm not looking at the body."

"You have to," said William. "How else are you going to find any clues? Are you just going to run your hands all over him like a blind person?"

Doyle looked ill. "No, I'm not going to do that, either. I'll stand outside the door."

"That's if we even get in," said Amanda. "It's dark inside. I bet dollars to donuts this door is locked."

She reached out and pulled.

"Yup," she said.

"Can we go through the main entrance and get to it that way?" asked Doyle. "If the morgue's closed up, maybe someone can let us in."

"It's worth trying," said William.

They walked around the building which took all of two minutes.

"Do they only have a dozen rooms in there?" asked Doyle.

"Shush, it's a small town," said Amanda. "I bet people rarely come here, anyway. Brainerd's not that far away."

"That begs the question," said William. "Why is the body here and not Brainerd?"

They approached the receptionist. She was a small, plump black woman with green scrubs on.

"Excuse me, are you a nurse?" asked William.

"Sometimes," she said. "For the next two hours I'm the receptionist."

"That's a little odd, isn't it?" said William.

"Not really. We have a staff of three tonight," she said.

"That's not much," said Doyle.

"We've had less," she said.

"Really?" Doyle said.

"Mmmhmm," the nurse/receptionist said. "Now what do you lovely people want this late in the evening?"

She eyed the group up and down. Her gaze landed on William in particular. Doyle wondered what she must think. His scruffy face, his white dress shirt only partly tucked in, red blood stain on the chest from the scuffle with Eva.

"Just so you know, we only give valid prescriptions for legitimate ailments, which must be signed by an M.D. We have one on staff tonight, and I assure you he does not hand them out like candy."

William seemed confused, but Doyle decided to jump ahead.

"Is the morgue open?" he asked.

The nurse/receptionist seemed taken aback. "What kind of sick, twisted people are—"

"We're nothing of the sort," said William, who glanced at Doyle and then added, "Mostly. You see, we're private detectives working on the Wilde case. We need to see the body to search for evidence."

"He was shot in the face. What kind of evidence could you possibly need?" she asked.

"Told ya," said Doyle, nudging William in the side.

"We just need to look. To be sure," said William. "Can we get access to the morgue?"

The nurse/receptionist shook her head. "I don't think so," she said. "He'll still be there in the morning. You should probably come back then."

"I'm sorry, ma'am, but this is extremely urgent. We cannot waste any time," said William. "Please, if you can, we truly need access to that morgue. You can watch us the entire time to assure we don't tamper with anything."

"Well, it has been rather boring in here tonight, and it would be something to do," she said. "But I still don't think so. I want to keep my job."

"Oh, really," said Doyle, reaching into his pocket. "Well, let's see what my good friend Abe Lincoln has to say about the matter." He dropped the bill onto the nurse/receptionist's desk.

"Five dollars?" she asked. "You want me to risk my job for five dollars?"

Doyle coughed. "Sorry, I thought that could go pretty far in a small town like this."

The nurse/receptionist grimaced at Doyle. "That's not very funny," she said.

Amanda apologized. "Really, he's not trying to be funny. He's just not all there."

"Hey . . ." Doyle said.

"Just kidding, sweetie," she said, then looked at the nurse/receptionist and mouthed, "I'm not."

"I tell you what," the nurse/receptionist said. "If I let you in there for a few minutes, *while I look on,*" she emphasized, "then will the three of you get the hell out of here and stop bothering me?"

They three detectives looked at each other. "Okay." "Sure." "Yup."

"This way, then," she said.

She led the detectives down a wide hallway past a few empty rooms and a corridor that led to the emergency operating room.

Doyle realized how eerily quiet it was for a hospital.

"Excuse me, miss . . . umm . . ." Doyle began.

"Babbit," she said. "Just call me Gina."

"Miss Babbit . . . Gina, thank you. Are there any, you know, patients here?" he asked.

"I'm guessing you've seen all the empty rooms. To be honest, we haven't had any patients here in the last three days, except for a couple kids who caught a stomach bug. Other than that, half the townspeople of Nisswa have already left for warmer temperatures. God forbid they see a single snowflake fall to the ground."

"So it's been quiet everywhere in town, not just the hospital?" asked William.

"Exactly. In fact, speaking of quiet," Gina said as she tapped the metal door behind her. "Here's the morgue."

As she said it, the door behind moved just a bit from her tapping.

"That's weird," said Gina.

"What's that?" asked Doyle, already feeling the heebie-jeebies he normally got whenever he was anywhere near blood, dead bodies, or clowns.

"Well, normally this door is locked when no one's attending to it. For some bizarre reason, it's open."

Doyle gulped.

Gina pushed the door open further, reached her hand within, and flicked a switch. Fluorescent lights illuminated the white linoleum tiled room. In the middle of the room stood a metal slab.

Doyle was shocked that a sheet-covered body was lying on the slab overnight. *Doesn't flesh usually decay if it's left out overnight? Like a carton of milk?* Doyle thought.

Then Doyle noticed, to his horror, that the sheet—the chest—was moving up and down in a rhythmic pattern.

"Oh, my God," said Amanda. "Is Wilde . . . alive?"

"Zoinks," said Doyle. "Let's get out of here."

Gina walked fearlessly into the room. "That can't be right," she said. "The body's supposed to be in the fridge. Let me check this out."

With abundant confidence that Doyle could barely imagine having, Gina approached the body, raised a forefinger, and poked it in the side.

A brief sputter was followed by a very vocal, "OW!"

There was an audible gasp as all three detectives were surprised by a noise coming from the obviously not-so-dead body.

"Dammit, Dewey—is that you?" asked Gina.

An arm appeared from under the sheet, reached up towards its face and—Doyle whimpered—pulled the sheet completely off its body. In the spot where Doyle was expecting to find a decaying, zombified corpse, a scrawny, silver-haired old man in green scrubs sat up suddenly.

"I wasn't sleeping, Gina, I swear to God in Heaven, I wasn't! I was working security, making sure no one busted in to the place."

Dewey looked around the room, dazed, as if he had just awoken from a long slumber.

"Oh, really? Is that a fact?" asked Gina.

"A couple hours ago, ya know, someone tried breakin' through the window there. Didn't break it or nothin', just tried to push it open. And I says, 'Hey, you burglar, you can't come in here,' and the person turned right around and left. Scared 'em off, I did. I'd do the same darn thing this very moment, if it came up," said Dewey, rubbing his eyes.

"Then why did I hear snoring?" said Gina.

Doyle had been too scared to hear it before, but now that she mentioned it . . .

"I thought you were a zombie!" exclaimed Doyle. Everyone in the room immediately turned to Doyle, a mixture of uneasiness and worry on their faces.

"Well, not literally . . ." said Doyle, back-pedaling.

"I'm not dead yet," said Dewey. "But I guess I did nod off there for a second or two . . ."

"Dewey, you can't be—" Gina began before William cut her off.

"Excuse me, Dewey," he said, "but could you describe the person who tried to get in here? Male/female, body shape, hair color . . . anything you can remember. Even shoes—shoes can be very important."

"Couldn't tell ya. He was wearin' all black. Top to bottom."

"So, it was a man, then?" asked William.

"Not positive," said Dewey. "Man-ish."

"What would you say about body shape?"

"Pretty average, I guess. Not chubby or nothin'."

"Anything peculiar or strange that you remember?" William asked.

"Nope . . . no, sir. This was an all-around average looking burglar. Yessir."

William grimaced. He wasn't getting much help.

"Did he or she say anything to you?" he asked.

"Nope, ran off pretty quick. I can be pretty intimidating, I suppose," said Dewey.

Gina put her arm around Dewey's shoulder and asked, "Unless these detectives have any further questions, don't you think you should head back to the supply room and keep working on inventory?"

Dewey looked around the room. "You guys are detectives?"

Doyle, William, and Amanda nodded.

"Wow, neat!" Dewey exclaimed. "I'd love to be a detective someday."

"Don't be ridiculous, Dewey," said Gina. "You're eighty-two years old."

"That may be so," said Dewey. "But I'm still hoping I'll get that 'Benjamin Button' disease. Sure'd be swell to be a young'un again."

"As long as you're young at heart," said Amanda, smiling at the old man affectionately.

"I'm not sure if you're aware of it, miss, but 'young at heart' doesn't ward off the grim reaper. That's why I work at this hospital here. See, way I figure it, everything's so clean here, I'm bound to stay healthy for a long time. And if I get sick, well, there's plenty of folks here to help me out. Right, Gina?"

"Sure, Dewey."

"Gina's really sweet once you get to know her," said Dewey. "Okay, I'll go do inventory now. Good-bye, detectives! Catch the burglar!"

"We're actually after the person who murdered Davis Wilde," said Doyle.

"Who?" asked Dewey.

"The actor," said Doyle.

"Oh, you mean the guy with the hole in his melon? He's in the icebox. Hold on a sec," he said, walking over to what looked like an oversized stainless-steel refrigerator. He pulled on the handle of a drawer which glided out with ease, revealing a body with a sheet tucked gently over it.

"Here you go, folks. Enjoy your evening," said Dewey, making his exit.

Amanda turned to Gina. "What a nice old man," she said.

Gina shook her head. "Honey, he's nice all right. But he's lost many of his marbles. Dewey's harmless, so we let him hang around the hospital all he wants. He even does a lot of work for us for free. A big help, actually. But he's been hearing and seeing things that aren't there. Like the burglar, for example. I bet you anything it was all in his head."

"Really?" asked William. "How certain are you? Keep in mind that this burglar could very well be Wilde's killer."

"If the burglar existed, which I doubt is the case," said Gina. "I'm sorry."

William nodded. "Very well."

"But I can point out something that might be helpful," said Gina.

"Yes? What would that be?" asked William.

"I know it probably wasn't even my business to look at Wilde— well, his body . . . but I did anyway. How could I resist? Not too many actors come into this hospital."

"I don't blame you," said Doyle. "So, let's get the obvious question out in the air. Was he well-endowed?"

Gina shook her head. "Apparently the rumors were false. But— check this out!"

Gina removed the sheet from the body's lower half, up to the thigh.

"Good God," said Doyle.

"What is that?" asked Amanda.

"Bite marks," said Gina. "All over his thighs. He may not have been big downstairs, but it looks like he still liked to get freaky."

"Freaky is right," said Doyle. "That looks like it would hurt pretty bad."

"I wouldn't try it," said Amanda.

"Good," said Doyle. "I'm glad that's out of the way."

"Are you two . . ." Gina asked.

"Almost," said Doyle and Amanda in unison, giving William a stern glare. William rolled his eyes.

"Do you realize what this might mean?" asked William. "This helps prove the murder was part of a love triangle gone awry, like I had originally suspected. Wonderful."

"So what do we do next?" asked Doyle.

William reached into his coat pocket and pulled out a small camera. "Let's start by taking snapshots of the bite marks. We may need to use them later to compare against the bite marks of various suspects. Gina, do you mind lifting up that sheet just a bit—"

Gina did as requested, but lifted the sheet just a bit too much, causing the sheet to slide off and fall to the floor, exposing the gaping, crusted hole in the center of Davis Wilde's forehead.

Doyle vomited directly onto the body. Onto Wilde's bare, inner thighs to be exact.

Gina covered her nose. "I'll get a mop," she said.

"Bloody hell, Doyle—I can't even see the bite marks now," said William.

"I'll get a rag," said Amanda.

"I need to go," said Doyle, white-faced, running as fast as possible for the nearest restroom.

William, left alone with the body, asked no one in particular, "Why did I make him my partner?"

10

Doyle woke up with a start.

"Are you okay?" asked Amanda, who was already sitting up in bed, her head resting against the wall.

Sweat dripped from Doyle's brow. He wrapped an arm around Amanda.

"Yeah, I think so," he said. "Creepy dream. That's all."

"Still have Wilde on your brain?" she asked.

"I have Wilde's brains on my brain," he said, then felt his stomach roll. "Let's talk about something else. Hey, what are you doing up? Did you have a bad dream, too?"

"No, I just couldn't sleep," she said.

"What've you been thinking about?" Doyle asked.

"What happened yesterday," she said.

"Listen, I know William interrupting us wasn't the most pleasant—" Doyle began.

"Not that," said Amanda. "The murder. Everything. I have a feeling it's more complicated than a simple love triangle."

"You do?" asked Doyle.

"I do. William thinks the bite marks are really important, and maybe they are, but it seems to me that Wilde has slept with many, many woman, possibly within the last month even, and any one of them could have bitten his thighs. I don't think that particular clue is going to amount to much."

"So, if this isn't a love triangle gone wrong," said Doyle, "then what's this all about?"

"Like every other crime, it's probably about money," she said.

"Really? You think so? But why?"

"I have no idea. But I bet you anything that when we get this figured out, money will have been a big factor," she said.

"But how can you be so sure with how little we know at this point?"

"Because—Wilde had money, and lots of other people don't."

Doyle shrugged. "Fair enough. So either way, you think this was a one-time killer?"

"Most likely," she said. "Unless the perp is still involved with the film, finds out we're on his or her trail, and decides to shoot us in the head, just like Wilde."

Doyle raised his eyebrows and sucked in his breath.

"I'm sure that's unlikely," said Amanda. "Don't worry. Really. Let's just investigate and find this person."

"Okay. Just stop saying stuff about us getting killed. I'm not a big fan of that, you know."

"I know, sorry. Should we get dressed and meet up with William?" she asked.

"Sure," said Doyle. "It's 7:00, so I'm sure William's up already. He usually doesn't sleep more than three hours, at least while he's on a case, anyway."

Amanda nodded, about to get out of bed when Doyle put his arm around her shoulder.

"Hey, you know—we could continue what we didn't finish yesterday . . ." Doyle said, massaging Amanda's back.

Amanda shook her head and stood up. "I don't think so. You still have a little bit of puke breath."

"Oh," said Doyle. "I can see how that would be a turn-off."

"Maybe later," said Amanda. "For now, let's try to keep our heads on the case."

It's about time," said William, leaning against the snow machine in Nisswa Park. "It's already 8:00. We could have been investigating for hours now."

"Sorry," said Doyle. "I had to brush my teeth a few times."

"No matter," said William. "So, I think the best place for us to start today is—"

"Hey, William," interrupted Doyle. "Where did you stay last night? I didn't see your car at the hotel."

"That's true," said Amanda. Then she gasped. "You didn't stay at . . ."

"Yes, yes—I stayed with Eva last night. We're trying to patch up some old wounds, you see."

"Uh-huh," said Amanda. "You realize she's a suspect, right?"

"Oh, stop with that nonsense," said William. "She called in the murder. And I happen to know her quite well."

"She called *you*, William—not the police. And the fact that she called anyone doesn't make her innocent."

"Are you telling me that you believe Eva is guilty of this crime?" asked William.

"Not at all," said Amanda. "I'm only saying that we need to treat her like any other suspect, because—whether you wish to acknowledge it or not—she *is* a suspect."

"Fine, fine—I'll stay at a hotel tonight. Let's just move on, shall we?"

"That's fine with me," said Doyle. "Hey, where is everyone?"

"Winthrop made an announcement an hour ago," said William. "Everyone's to remain on set, although there won't be any filming today. Therefore, almost everyone is at the catering table."

"So, how should we proceed here?" asked Doyle.

"It sounds like Maura Coen, the director, is ready to speak with us this morning. In fact, Winthrop said she planned on meeting me, right here, in about ten minutes."

"Do you think she's a likely suspect?" asked Amanda.

"Well, I can't imagine most directors would want to have their lead actor killed midway through filming," said William. "Although, this could be an unusual situation. I think we're better off treating her like a primary suspect until we feel otherwise."

"Sounds fair enough," said Doyle.

"However, I think it's good to keep in mind—" As William spoke, he moved slightly against the snow machine, his lower back pushing against something small and round that made a small clicking sound. Within a split second, torrents of white powdery snow blasted like a fire hose directly at Doyle's chest.

Doyle made an "uff" sound as he was knocked several feet back. He lay still as white snow piled on top of him.

"What did I . . ." said William, as he looked at the machine.

"Doyle!" shouted Amanda, running to his side and pulling him by the arms out of the oncoming blast of snow.

She brushed the snow off his face with her bare hands. His eyes were closed.

"Doyle, are you okay?"

He opened his mouth. Then his eyes opened, too.

"Doyle?"

"Ooooow!" yelled Doyle. "That really hurt!"

"Sorry," said William. "I didn't realize . . ."

"Let's take a look," said Amanda. She unbuttoned Doyle's shirt and opened it. Already it showed signs of bruising and swelling.

"This doesn't look very good," said Amanda. "You might want to have a doctor check you out."

"I'm fine," said Doyle. "Snow can't affect me. I'm a Minnesotan."

"You better not be wrecking my machine," said a stern voice from behind them.

The three detectives turned their heads towards the voice.

"Of course, it may not do much good if we can't get this film up and running again," she said.

"Maura Coen, I presume?" asked William.

"That's correct. I'm the director of this disaster. Now, what is it you want with me?"

"I'm sorry, Ms. Coen, but it seems we're bothering you. I assumed you would want to help the three of us—including the detective who was just seriously hurt on your set—to find the person who killed your lead actor yesterday."

"Pardon my lack of enthusiasm. The truth is, whether you catch this man or not, it's not going to change the fact that my movie is ruined."

"Aren't you interested in justice?" asked William. "To see the man who destroyed your film go down?"

"No, detective. I don't care about that. I just want to make my fucking movie. My goddamn brothers are going to be thrilled about this. They've told me time and time again that I'll never be able to make a blockbuster film. They don't think I have the head for it. When they hear about this . . . oh, God. I hate to think of it."

"Haven't you considered filing a civil suit against the person who caused this?" asked William.

Maura Coen paused. "I can do that?"

"Of course," said William. "If the murder causes the collapse of the movie, they're ultimately responsible for the cost."

"I didn't consider that," she said. "Hmm."

Maura Coen looked around her.

"There's something you should know," she said. She pointed at Doyle. "Put your shirt back on. I need you three to follow me."

"Where are we going?" asked Amanda.

"To my trailer," said Maura. "I have information that I don't want prying ears to hear."

Doyle buttoned his shirt and stood up, melted snow dripping from his clothes.

"I could have died from that, you know."

Maura shook her head. "I don't think so. Toughen up, chicken legs."

Doyle looked down. "Hey, they're not—"

"Just follow me," she said, leading the detectives down a trail towards the campers and trailers.

They walked in silence as they followed Maura down a path, around a group of trees, towards a small, enclosed area that contained an enormous RV.

"Do you live in this thing?" asked Doyle, rubbing his battered chest.

"No," said Maura, "but I film a ton, so it's practical for me to have something like this, that can take me wherever I need to go. When I'm not filming, I live in Los Angeles, with all the other big-name directors."

"You've made other movies?" asked Doyle.

Maura Coen glared at Doyle with contempt. "Yes, Detective, I've filmed several other movies, each of which are famous in their own right. Clearly you know nothing of the movie industry. Now get inside."

As Maura entered her temporary home and the detectives brought up the rear, Doyle whispered to Amanda, "I don't like her."

Once everyone settled into the mammoth-sized vehicle, William said, "Not that I'm trying to be pushy, madam, but we have an awful lot of investigating to do. I do hope you'll get right to the point."

"Absolutely, Detective. I also have a lot of work to do, and I cannot wait for the lot of you to get off my set. No offense."

"Certainly," said William. "Now, if you don't mind, what is this critical information that you didn't want anyone to hear?"

"Well," she said, looking in all directions and over her shoulder, even though it was clear that no one else was in the RV except for Maura herself and the detectives. "I've gotten solid information from members of the cast and crew that the producer—I'm not sure if you've met him yet, but his name is Ronald Winthrop—anyways, I've received information that he been engaging in sordid activities with Tina Callahan, the make-up artist."

William smiled and chuckled. "Thank you for that, Ms. Coen, but we've already heard and disregarded the rumors that Mr. Winthrop and Ms. Callahan were having relations."

Maura Coen shook her head. "No, no—not with each other. With Davis Wilde, my dead lead actor."

This information caused a palpable stir in the room.

"Both of them . . . with Wilde?" asked Doyle. "Really?"

"That's right, Detective Malloy."

William readied his notepad and pen. "Ms. Coen, you said you had proof. What sort of proof do you have regarding this?"

"Well, almost everyone working on this production will give you the same information. Everyone saw the three of them walking in together."

William threw down the pen.

"Not only is that not admissible evidence whatsoever, but every person we've spoken to thus far has said that they've seen Tina Callahan and Ronald Winthrop walk into Winthrop's trailer for extended periods of time. So far, you're the only one that's brought Wilde into the mix."

"I imagine that's because Wilde wanted to be discreet. I have photographs, if that helps," said Maura Coen.

William picked up his pen. "Finally, some actual evidence . . ."

Maura took a key out of her pocket and opened a filing cabinet she had next to her small, fold-down bed. She reached in and grabbed a handful of Polaroids and passed them around the room.

"Eww," said Doyle. "I really didn't need to see this."

"Wait a minute," said Amanda. "This looks like two women with Wilde."

"Yes and no," said Maura. "That's Winthrop in the blonde wig."

"Eww," repeated Doyle.

"Ms. Coen, can I ask you why you have these Polaroids?" asked William.

"Someone handed them to me," she said. "Someone who was concerned about the production."

"I take it you're intentionally not revealing your source?" asked William.

"I promised this person I wouldn't let anyone know," she said firmly.

"You know, whoever gave you these photos could be the murderer," said William. "They may have been trying to blackmail Wilde, and the whole thing went wrong. There are a number of possibilities."

"That may be so, but I have total confidence in this person. If you rule out all other possibilities, then maybe. But until then, I'll say nothing."

"Okay," said William. "So you think that perhaps either Tina Callahan or Ronald Winthrop, because they're involved in these vulgar acts, may be responsible for the murder?"

Maura Coen shook her head. "Not at all," she said. "I'm only showing you these photos because there's someone else in that room. That person is the murderer. I'd bet my reputation as a director on it."

Doyle rolled his eyes. Amanda nudged him.

"Look, Doyle—she's right. Look in the corner of this one."

"You're right—that's definitely dark brown hair . . . maybe black. Who is that?"

"The woman who's been one inch from Wilde since she arrived in Brainerd. Eva Wong."

William stood up with a start. "That's impossible and you know it!" he said, sharply. William yanked the photo out of Amanda's hand and put it in front of Maura's face. He pointed at the hair in question. "This could be anyone, Ms. Coen. This could even be you. Why should we take your word on this?"

"Because, from what I can tell, this is the best information you have. Eva Wong's been around him the past few days. Always nearby, staring, but never speaking. I should have known something was wrong and called in extra security, the authorities, something . . ."

"She was not involved in this!" blurted William.

"I think you're right," Maura said. "I don't think she was involved in the sexual escapades. But she was sitting there, watching everything. Isn't that even more off-putting than actually be involved in the act?"

"LISTEN HERE," William began shouting until Doyle yanked him from behind and pulled him all the way out of the RV.

Amanda turned to Maura and said, "Thanks for the information."

Maura nodded .

"WILLIAM, YOU CAN'T DO THAT," said Doyle. "I know you're personally involved with the case, which is making you, you know, extra passionate. But you can't let your personal feelings interfere with how we're conducting this investigation. Whether you like it or not, Eva is a suspect—" William was about to interject when Doyle stopped him. "—Eva is a suspect *until* we verify who the real killer is, or until we verify that Eva could not have possibly been involved."

"She couldn't have been involved," said William.

"You know what I mean, William. "Evidence is key here. Find the right evidence, and you can make Maura Coen eat her words."

William nodded. "You're right. Thank you, Doyle. I just need to keep my wits about me, be methodical, and find the real perpetrator. I can see now I'm getting all worked up for nothing."

Doyle hesitantly said, "You're welcome. Are you sure you're okay, William?"

"Just fine. Really, it was just too many emotions. I'll be okay. I swear."

"Good," said Doyle. "That's great."

"Yes," said William. "It is good. Isn't it?"

"Yes," said Doyle. "Very good."

Amanda stepped out from the RV. "Since that pleasant scene is over now, what are we doing next?" she asked.

"Well, I guess—" began Doyle.

"I'll be going for a walk," William said, suddenly.

"A walk?" asked Amanda.

"Yes, Amanda. Just a nice, brisk walk. A little exercise is good for the soul," he said.

"Where are you going to walk?" asked Amanda.

"Oh, around the park, I suppose," said William. "Many beautiful trees this time of year."

"That's good," said Amanda.

"We've already gone through all that," said Doyle. "Enjoy your walk, William. Call me in a half hour, okay?"

William seemed to think about it for a moment before saying, "Yes, I will call you, Doyle. I will definitely do that."

Doyle and Amanda gave each other a nervous glance.

"Bye, William," said Doyle.

"Ciao," said William.

12

manda and Doyle approached the catering table and its wondrous spread of pastries, fruits, cereals, and muffins, as well as coffee, orange juice, and milk.

"Thank God," said Doyle. "I'm starving."

They both piled their plates high and found a boulder near the lake to sit down.

"Is William going to be okay?" Amanda asked.

Doyle shook his head. "I'm not sure. Granted, I've only known him for a couple weeks, mostly while we worked on the last case. But I've definitely never seen him act like this. That's for sure."

"Relationships can be tricky," said Amanda. "Especially when murder might be involved."

"You've gone through this before?" asked Doyle.

"Maaaaybe," she said, putting her hands around his neck and squeezing.

Doyle began coughing and wheezing.

"I'm sorry, Doyle—are you okay? I was only pretending to kill you."

He gasped. "It's okay. I had half a raspberry Danish in my mouth. If it weren't for that, it would have been very cute and funny."

She laughed. "Sorry about that."

"It's fine."

After a couple minutes of munching, Doyle said, "I really can't imagine what William is going through right now. I can't imagine what it would be like to think, or even hear allegations, that your significant other is a stone-cold murderer. It's creepy."

"It's sad," said Amanda. "I've only known him for a short while, too. But he seemed so strong and confident to me. Now, he's falling apart."

"He doesn't have anyone to lean on," said Doyle. "Except us. That can't be too comforting."

Amanda put an arm around him. "We're not that bad," she said.

"Speak for yourself, Officer Hutchins. You gonna eat that pineapple spear?"

Doyle was in the process of grabbing the fruit off her plate when Amanda said, "Doyle, isn't that—"

Doyle looked in the direction Amanda was pointing.

"You're right. That's the effects guy. What's his name . . . Chip?"

"Yes, that's it," she said. "He's really piling up the pastries."

Doyle took a bite of pineapple. He looked at Amanda. Then he looked at Chip.

"Come with me," he said.

"What? What are you doing? Should we wait for William?"

"I think it's safe to say we're on our own, now. I really don't think William will be much assistance to us, at least not for a while."

Amanda nodded. "Okay, let's go."

Once again, Doyle and Amanda approached the catering table. Doyle tapped Chip's shoulder.

"WHA!?" Chip shrieked, sending a plateful of pastries flying in all directions.

"You okay, there?" asked Doyle. "Chip was the name, right?"

Chip was suddenly breathing heavily. "That's correct, Officer. How can I help you?"

"I already told you, Chip. I'm not an officer, I'm a detective. A private investigator. Ms. Hutchins, by my side here, however, is an officer. So she gets all the toys. You know, guns, handcuffs, mace, one of those sticks she uses to beat people with . . ."

"Only when necessary," said Amanda.

"Usually, sure," said Doyle.

Chip made an audible whimper.

"Do you mind if I run through a couple quick questions with you, Chip?"

"Uhh, yeah, sure. No problem," he said.

"Looks like you dropped your pastries," said Doyle. "Would you care to get a new one?"

"Nah," he said. "I'm not really hungry."

"Okay," said Doyle. "Whatever you say."

"Can we go somewhere private?" he asked. "There's an awful lot of people around here."

"Somewhere private. That's a good idea," said Doyle. "Somewhere private . . . let's see, how about Winthrop's trailer? How does that sound?"

"What? Why there?" asked Chip.

"Well, you've been there before, haven't you? Took a few photos, did ya?" asked Doyle.

"NO!" Chip yelled. "I mean yes! I mean . . . why do you ask?"

"Are you sure you don't want a donut?" asked Doyle.

"Yeah, a little bit," said Chip. "Are you arresting me? Is this my last meal?"

Amanda shrugged.

Doyle seemed to think about it for a moment. "Not quite yet. There's still so much we need to know."

"Who told you, anyways? Was it Ms. Coen? She's such a bad person. You know?"

"No, I don't know, Chip. But what I want to know is why you spent your evenings spying on people having sex rather than getting your beauty sleep."

"The Internet barely works up here," said Chip.

"Okay . . ." said Doyle. "And . . . ?"

"So, I couldn't see any . . . you know," he said.

"Any what?" asked Doyle.

Chip spelled it out. "P O R N"

"It's too bad I can't spell, because then I would know what you're talking about," said Amanda, shaking her head angrily.

"Sorry . . . sorry, miss. I'm not good with women. I guess that's why I was using my Polaroid camera in the first place. If anything, I figured the photos might be worth a few bucks on the internet. But once Davis Wilde was shot, well, then I knew I needed to turn in the photographs, but I didn't want to be tied with them. That's why I gave them to Ms. Coen. I figured that way, she could turn them to the authorities without getting me involved. She promised me."

"Clearly, it didn't turn out well," said Doyle, "regardless of your good and perverted intentions."

"Chip, did you see Eva Wong in Winthrop's trailer?" asked Amanda.

He shook his head. "No, I only saw Davis, Tina, and Mr. Winthrop. I'm pretty sure I would have remembered Eva Wong being in there. She's very attractive." He felt the glare of Amanda's eyes. "You know, so to speak."

"Ms. Coen gave us the impression that Eva was in Mr. Winthrop's trailer during the sexual tryst, looking on. Is it possible she was in the trailer but mostly out of view? All we have is one photograph that shows the back of her head."

"I guess it's possible," said Chip. "I think I would have noticed that, but maybe not."

"Did you notice any of them leaving the trailer?" asked Doyle.

"No, I didn't stick around that long," said Chip. "But, now that you bring this up, I did notice Ms. Wong was strangely fascinated with Wilde. I mean, the other days on set. I couldn't tell if she thought he was hot, or if it was something more than that."

"But you did notice some sort of attraction between Eva and Wilde?"

Chip nodded. "Yes, definitely."

Doyle glanced at Amanda to see if she had any more questions for Chip. She shook her head.

"Thank you, Chip. This information could be very helpful," said Doyle.

"Am I under arrest?" asked Chip.

Amanda pulled out her handcuffs, then Doyle waved them away.

"No, that won't be necessary . . . this time. Make sure you stick around. No funny business. Or else. Got it?"

Chip nodded nervously. The half-eaten donut on his plate bounced up and down, then landed on the floor.

"Careful with the pastries, Chip," said Doyle. "Those things can kill you."

"Yes, sir," he said.

"Have a lovely day," said Doyle. Amanda followed behind him.

"Can I have the photos back?" Chip called out from the catering table.

Amanda turned around first. "Really? You want to go there?"

"No, ma'am," he hollered back. "Sorry. Sorry again. Thank you."

13

William Wright waited patiently behind a tree so Doyle and Amanda wouldn't see him. As they moseyed towards the catering table in the distance, William stealthily moved into a wide cluster of trailers.

He already knew which one he was looking for. He'd slept in it last night.

William knocked on the door. Loudly. Rapidly.

The door opened. "What is it? What's going on? Is everyone okay?" Eva asked.

"Everything's fine, just fine. I'm just having a terrible day, sweetheart."

"I haven't even finished my first coffee of the day, and you've already had a terrible day?"

"It's just that . . . we talked to Maura, and—"

"Well, there's your problem right there," said Eva. "If you want to have a terrible day, talk to Maura Coen."

"Yes, well—there's just so many rumors flying around, and I just can't believe—"

"Let me guess. You've heard rumors that I could be the killer. You've been involved with me—"

"I *am* involved with you."

"Right. But you've never thought of me as a suspect before, and you're having trouble coping with it."

"You know you're a suspect?"

"Of course I am. I was on set that day. Besides—it's the film industry. Ridiculous rumors fly around all the time. It's silly. And I'm certain you haven't seen any evidence to suggest I'm the killer, right?"

William thought of the photo. The one with her hair. Just because she was in that room didn't mean she killed Wilde, right? Preposterous.

"No, I've seen nothing," said William. "Just a lot of rumors." He laughed. "Oh, I feel absolutely loony. But you were in the trailer, right? Why were you there? It really doesn't matter, I guess. I'm just curious."

"What trailer? What are you talking about?" asked Eva.

"You know, the umm . . . orgy."

Eva's jaw just about dropped to the ground.

"What . . . orgy . . . are you talking about William?"

"You've been to more than one?" asked William, shocked.

"I haven't been to *any* orgies, thank you very much!" exclaimed Eva. "Why, what orgy have you heard about? Better call *Entertainment Tonight*. This sounds juicy."

Eva crossed her arms.

"Well?" she asked.

"Umm . . . another silly rumor, I guess," said William. "There's just been an awful lot going around about you and Wilde—it's all rather ludicrous, I suppose."

"What sort of rumors?"

"Oh, you know—that you were incredibly attracted to him, that you wanted to be around him every waking moment. You know, et cetera et cetera."

"I won't deny that I was extremely attracted to Davis Wilde. Have you seen him with his shirt off?"

William thought of the morgue. And Doyle's vomit.

"Yes, actually," said William.

"So you understand, then, that it's not unusual to be attracted to . . . a body like that."

"I don't really want to hear this," said William, looking away.

"I was never *with* him, though," said Eva. "I haven't been with anyone since you."

Their eyes connected.

"Really?" asked William.

Eva nodded. "I thought you might like to know."

William sighed. "I did want to know. Thank you."

"So don't listen to these rumors that turn a simple attraction into, apparently, an orgy. Okay?"

"Yes, yes of course. I'm so sorry. I feel like such an idiot."

"Well, sometimes you can be," said Eva. "I know you've seen some terrible things. Back in London. And I know that leads you to suspect the worst in people. But you have to trust some people. Especially the ones closest to you."

"You're right," said William. "I'll never second-guess you again. I love you, Eva."

"I love you, too. Do you want to come in? I've made a fresh pot of coffee."

"No, no that's okay. I feel . . . reinvigorated. I feel confident again. I just need to trust my instincts. They've done well for me so far. I just need to trust them."

"You got it. Go ahead, William. Find who killed Wilde. He may not have been the nicest guy around, but he didn't deserve to die like that."

"Fair enough," said William. "Can I see you tonight?"

"I doubt we'll be filming anytime soon, so I should be available."

"Wonderful."

"I'll see you tonight, William."

"Good-bye, Eva," William said, kissing her delicately on the cheek.

14

Doyle drove slowly down the two-lane highway from Nisswa Park to their hotel. It was Friday afternoon, so traffic was starting to build with travelers coming up from the Twin Cities to their cabins up north.

"You know, Chip could have killed Wilde," said Amanda.

"Why?" asked Doyle.

"He took photographs of a strange sexual encounter, then someone —probably Wilde himself—saw Chip snapping the photos. I don't know what happened then. Maybe Wilde threatened Chip. I mean, Chip has been overly nervous this entire time. Maybe he put the real bullets in the gun because he was scared of Wilde. It's possible."

"You might be right," said Doyle. "But I'm not so sure. Chip's been nervous, but he doesn't seem like a killer to me. Even if he was scared."

"Who else then?" asked Amanda. "This has to be tied to those photographs somehow."

"Not necessarily," said Doyle. "I have a feeling that Wilde has been in sexual orgies before, and that this wasn't the first time he was photographed. He's from Hollywood. People there do that sort of thing."

"How do you know?" asked Amanda.

"Have you ever gone to YouTube? They have *everything* there," said Doyle.

"Oh," said Amanda. "Gotcha."

Doyle honked his horn. "C'mon," he said. "I can't believe how bad traffic is today."

"It's the weekend," said Amanda. "Not much you can do about it."

"Sure there is," said Doyle. "Open up the glove box."

Amanda did, and something dark red and boxy fell out onto the car floor.

"What the hell?"

"Hand that to me," said Doyle.

Amanda held it up. "Why do you still have this?"

"A little memento from the MPD," said Doyle. He took it from her and placed it on the top of his car. Within seconds, the top of the car was flashing and Doyle was driving down the shoulder.

"You really shouldn't be doing this," said Amanda. "Not only are you not a Brainerd cop, but you're no longer a cop at all. You could get in some serious trouble here."

"Oh, don't worry—you're a cop. See, it all works out nicely."

Amanda shrugged. "Well, at least we'll be at the hotel soon."

"Why are we going there, anyway?" asked Doyle.

"I forgot my Blackberry. I needed to look up a few things," she said.

"All righty," said Doyle.

After two miles of driving down the shoulder, they arrived at the hotel.

"That didn't take long," said Amanda.

"Exactly," said Doyle. "Should I just wait here?"

"Naw, why don't you come up and help me look. I can't remember where I left it."

"Oh, sure—no problem," he said.

WHEN THEY APPROACHED THE DOOR to their room, which still had a sizeable hole from William's gun, they discovered a not-so-friendly looking envelope with their room number written across the front taped to the door.

"I imagine hotel management is not so happy about the door," said Doyle.

"Why don't you just give that to William and let him take care of it," said Amanda.

"I like that idea," said Doyle and left the envelope taped to the door.

Doyle kicked the door, and it swung open. "So, where do you think you left the Blackberry?" asked Doyle.

Amanda closed the door behind them. "I don't have a Blackberry," she said.

Doyle turned around and gave her a questioning look.

"What—"

"Well, we got interrupted yesterday, and William's occupied, so I figured this might be a good time to . . ."

Doyle gasped. "Officer Hutchins!"

"Oh, shut up, Doyle," she said. "We should probably make this fast. We do have a lot of work to do."

"Fast is the only way I know how!" said Doyle.

They embraced and kissed far more passionately than the preceding conversation would suggest. Within moments they were on the bed, then they were fumbling with each other's belts, and then, finally, they were making love.

Suddenly, the door burst open with a violent crash.

"Doyle, Amanda—are you okay!?" yelled the unmistakable voice of William.

Doyle and Amanda shrieked simultaneously, and a millisecond later, William shrieked as well.

"Good Lord, do you people ever wear clothes?" he yelled, then darted out of the room.

Doyle and Amanda looked at each other, then each muttered a cornucopia of expletives the likes of which were rarely heard in Brainerd.

15

Doyle and Amanda walked fully clothed into the hotel hallway. William's face was rigid, like stone. He didn't even turn his head to look at them.

"Whoa, William—we're sorry. I know that probably wasn't the prettiest sight, but no need to be upset with us," said Doyle.

William was holding the envelope taped to their door.

"How could you go in there and do . . . *that* . . . and completely ignore this death threat?"

"Death threat!?" Doyle and Amanda exclaimed.

"Didn't you read it?" asked William.

"No," said Doyle. "I'm sorry, William—I guess we should have. What does it say?"

"It says 'Call off the investigation or E.W. disappears.' Someone wants to kill Eva." said William, looking down at his shoes. Doyle suspecting he was suppressing a tidal wave of anger.

Amanda took the note from William. "Weird. The letters and words are cut from newspapers. I didn't know people actually did that—I thought it was just a movie thing."

"It might not mean Eva," said Doyle. "E.W. could mean anything."

Before William could speak, Amanda said, "I'm pretty sure it means Eva. It would be awfully obscure if whoever was doing this was planning to take down *Entertainment Weekly*."

"Good point," said Doyle.

"We have to do something," said William. "We just made up. I can't let her be killed by some maniac."

"She'll be fine, William," said Amanda.

"We have to call off the investigation," said William.

"No . . . I don't think that's the right way to go here," said Doyle. "If it was anyone but Eva, you definitely wouldn't stop the investigation, would you William?"

"No, but it *is* Eva. I've never had a case become this personal," said William.

"Listen, William—I hate bringing this up again, I really do—but you have to remember that Eva is still a suspect. She could have written this note."

A fire burned in William's eyes. Doyle had never seen anything like it.

"She did not write the note. She explained her side of everything this morning," said William.

Amanda attempted to calm him down.

"You're probably right, William. Frankly, I'm leaning towards the Chip guy," she said.

William's stern look eased a bit.

"Did Eva say anything about the photographs?" asked Amanda.

William nodded. "She said she wasn't there."

"All right. Did she say anything else?"

"No, but she didn't have to. Listen, this letter is a threat against her. I need to go to her right now. She needs protection."

Amanda wrapped her arm around William. "I understand how you're feeling right now, but you're running on impulse and that's not going to help us. Now, you know that Eva is a very strong woman. In fact, she was kicking in your testicles just yesterday. Do you really think she's all that vulnerable?"

"No, I suppose not," William replied.

"When we were talking just now, we brought up again the possibility that Eva could potentially allegedly maybe possibly be the criminal. But we're not saying she is the criminal. As detectives, we cannot exclude her from the investigation. Do you agree with that?"

William nodded. "I do."

"And do you also agree that someone was murdered yesterday, and whoever did it needs to be brought to justice before they can do it again to someone else?"

"Yes," said William.

"Good. Will you forget about the fact that you saw me and Doyle being intimate in that room?"

"No, probably not," he said, and chuckled.

"Excellent—I guess we're all on the same page now. Right, guys?"

Doyle and William nodded.

"Yeah, definitely," said Doyle.

"So what do we do now?" asked William.

"Well," said Amanda. "I suggest we form a plan."

"Preferably a good one," said Doyle.

"As long as we can keep an eye on Eva and make sure she's okay," said William. "You understand that if anything happens, I will hold all three of us responsible."

Without a hesitation, Amanda responded, "We won't let anything happen to her, William."

"You know, if we can help it," said Doyle.

Amanda nudged Doyle.

"Ow," he said. "I mean, there's absolutely no way anything bad is ever going to happen to her, ever."

"Right," said William. "Let's just get back to the park, shall we?"

"Okay," said Doyle.

Within seconds, they piled into Doyle's car and merged into traffic.

16

hat's going on?" asked Doyle, as he parked the car in the unexpectedly crowded lot. "Who is that?"

"My guess would be the chief of police," said Amanda.

"What makes you say that?" asked Doyle.

"Because he looks like Chief Burnside, but with a mustache."

Doyle glanced at the man at the podium a second time. He was flipping through note cards, beads of sweat glistening on his brow.

"You're right, he does look like Burnside," said Doyle. "But what is Brainerd's chief of police doing here?"

"Probably a press release on Wilde's murder. It had to happen sometime," said Amanda.

A good-sized crowd had gathered around the podium, which appeared to include most of the film's cast and crew as well as many local residents and media types.

Amanda and Doyle got out of the car, followed closely by William.

"She won't answer her phone," William muttered.

"Maybe she can't hear it," said Doyle. "There are an awful lot of people here. Just look around."

William nodded. "Yes, okay. I'm going to look for her." He immediately darted into the crowd as the police chief began speaking.

"Ladies and gentlemen," the Brainerd chief of police said in a gruff, no-nonsense voice, "the reason for this press conference is two-fold. One, a freak accident on the set of a film in production on the outskirts of Brainerd in Nisswa Park claimed the life of famed and beloved actor Davis Wilde."

"Accident?" said Doyle. Amanda also looked confused by the statement.

"Two," continued the chief, "Actress Eva Wong, also working on the same film, was kidnapped from her trailer less than three hours ago."

With this, the crowd erupted. Doyle had lost sight of William.

"Everyone, please. I will answer your questions one at a time," said the chief.

"I can't believe she was kidnapped," said Amanda. "Whoever wrote that note didn't even give us a chance."

"I know," said Doyle. "Let's hear what this guy has to say."

A reporter from the local Fox station raised his hand. "Sir, are these two events related?"

The chief shook his head. "We don't have enough information at this time to determine that."

"What specifically happened to Davis Wilde?" another reporter asked.

"A faulty prop. That's all we can say at this time."

Another hand was raised. "How do you know Ms. Wong was kidnapped?"

"Her trailer was trashed, and blood was . . ." the chief coughed . . . "everywhere."

The crowd erupted once again, but within seconds, a voice rose above the roar of the reporters, the film crew, and the townspeople. It was the voice of William, crying out.

The noise died down until only William's voice was audible.

"Poor guy," said Amanda. "He's not taking the news well."

"That has nothing to do with it," said Doyle. "I think he's in pain."

Sure enough, the crowd drew away from William, who was lying on the ground, curled up in the fetal position. Blood was flowing out from his side.

"Oh, my God . . ." said Amanda. Doyle was already running towards him.

17

The events that followed happened so fast that Doyle was barely able to register them. Doyle was naked except for a loose-fitting pair of box shorts. This is because he'd taken off his shirt and wrapped it around William's abdomen. Then he'd taken off his belt and wrapped it around the shirt to secure it and add some needed pressure onto the wound. Without the belt holding up his pants, Doyle's last substantial piece of clothing fell to the ground.

"William, who did this?" asked Doyle.

"I don't know," said William, panting. "Too many people around. Couldn't see."

William squirmed on the ground.

"Why are you naked?" he asked.

"You really shouldn't move, William. And I'm not naked. As you can see, I'm wearing undershorts."

"But why . . . ?"

"I'm saving your life," said Doyle.

"I don't understand," said William.

"Just . . . try to heal."

"Things are getting interesting," said Amanda, who finally pushed her way through the hordes of people. Her eyes grew wide when she saw William squirming on the ground.

"How so?" asked Doyle.

"They just closed off the exit so no one can leave, and if I heard the chief of police correctly, they'll have about a jillion squad cars here in no time."

"Hmm, that does change things some," said Doyle.

"Possibly for the worse," said Amanda. "Now they're definitely not going to want us working on this case, especially since one of our own is a victim."

William grabbed Amanda's hand. "I don't care who killed Wilde," he said, wincing, "or even who stabbed me. Just get Eva . . ."

"We will, William. Don't worry," said Doyle. "Oh, and you owe me twenty bucks for a new shirt."

William waved him away with a flick of his hand.

The ambulance pulled in much faster than Doyle thought it would.

"William—just relax," said Doyle. "Stop worrying about Eva and just try to heal. We have the situation under control."

"I'll stop worrying about Eva as soon as she's safe," said William.

The paramedics hustled Doyle and Amanda away, and within minutes, William was loaded onto a stretcher and carted away from Nisswa Park.

Amanda pulled Doyle away from the crowd of gawkers.

"This is getting really weird," said Amanda.

"What do you mean?" asked Doyle, momentarily forgetting that he was wearing nothing but underwear and sparsely sprinkled chest hair.

"Things are happening really fast, and I'm afraid we're overlooking important details," said Amanda.

"Like what, for example?"

"The note on our motel room door," she said. "Do you think it's likely someone had time to drive to the motel, post the threatening message, drive all the way back, and then kidnap Eva? What was the point of the threat if the perpetrator was planning on doing it anyway?"

Doyle stared blankly into space. Finally he looked at her and asked, "So what does that mean?"

"It means we're probably dealing with two people here," she said, arms crossed.

"Crap," said Doyle. "That complicates things. I *hate* that."

"It'll be all right," said Amanda. "We'll figure it out. We just have to pick up the pace. Eva is in some serious danger."

"Unless she's one of the two," said Doyle.

"It's possible," she said. "But for William's sake, I hope she's innocent. He seems awfully fragile right now. I'm not sure he could handle it."

"He'll be fine," said Doyle. "Did you see how well he handled that knife wound? William's a strong dude."

"He's also a lucky dude," said Amanda. "And it pisses me off to no end that whoever stabbed him was in the crowd, and apparently no one saw anything."

"Can we get a full list of everyone here? Can we get the police to walk around and collect names?"

"That won't be any help," said Amanda. "Too much time has passed. They sealed off the exits, but there's a whole damn forest back there. Whoever wielded the knife could have made it out. Especially by now."

"I guess," said Doyle. "So how the heck do we figure this out?"

"Let's dig around," said Amanda. "Starting with Eva's trailer."

"OH, GOD," SAID DOYLE, TRYING HIS BEST not to look at the trail of blood that led from Eva's bed to the door.

"I know," said Amanda. "I feel terrible for her, too."

"No, it's not that. It's just so . . . red," Doyle said, then quickly exited the trailer to breathe in some fresh air.

"Puh-leeze," said Amanda. "There's probably only a cup's worth of blood in here. That's nothing. The white carpet makes the blood appear a little exaggerated, that's all. Get back in here."

"Okay," said Doyle as he re-entered. "Do we know for sure if this is Eva's blood?"

"No, I don't think so. And I bet the police can't be sure, either. I should talk to them, see if they're running any tests."

"Knick-knacks have been knocked over, but nothing's really broken. I don't think we can say with any degree of certainty that there was a struggle in here," said Doyle.

"Or it's a faux-struggle put upon by someone who didn't actually want to break any of her possessions," said Amanda.

"Or someone snuck up on her, bashed her on the head, thus not giving her much of an opportunity to flail around and knock things over, save a few figurines."

"Certainly a possibility," said Amanda.

Both of them scratched their chins as they looked around the small space.

"But there's gotta be something we're missing . . ." said Doyle.

"Like Eva, perhaps?" said Amanda, dryly.

A commotion coming from outside the trailer caused Amanda to step outside, yanking Doyle along with her.

"Something's happening," Amanda said.

"Where is everyone running?" asked Doyle.

"That way," she said. "Let's go."

18

As Doyle and Amanda approached the bustling crowd several yards into the thick of the forest, they couldn't tell exactly what everyone was looking at. Then as they got closer, they saw: long, dark hair, a white hood, and then finally her face. It was Eva.

"Oh, no . . ." said Amanda.

Doyle grabbed her shoulder, and together they pushed through the gawkers. "Check her pulse," he said.

They both kneeled down by Eva. Doyle explored her head for serious injury.

"She's still alive," said Amanda. "Do you see anything?"

"No, nothing," said Doyle. "I don't see any blood on her head anywhere."

People were shouting from behind. "What's happening?" "What's wrong with her?" "Will she be okay?"

Doyle held his palm out, asking for silence.

"Eva!" Doyle yelled directly at the unconscious woman's face. "Eva, are you in there?"

He heard more murmurs. "What's he trying to do?" "Is he a policeman?"

"EVA! It's me, Doyle! William's buddy. You remember William, right?"

"Seriously, Doyle—what are you doing?" asked Amanda.

"I'm not really sure. I thought this might work," said Doyle. "Not to worry. I'm not out of ideas quite yet."

Doyle cracked his knuckles.

"EVA! ARISE!" Doyle shouted, as he slapped Eva across the face.

Doyle felt arms grab him by the armpits and lift him up to his feet.

"What the—" Doyle muttered as he spun around to face an angry-looking man in uniform.

"Sir, just what in the h-e-double hockey sticks do you think you're doing?" the policeman asked.

Before he could speak, Amanda piped in. "Sorry, Officer . . . Daniels. We were just trying to awaken Ms. Wong."

Officer Daniels looked at Doyle directly. "By slapping her?"

"We use that method in the Twin Cities all the time," he said.

"You're a cop?" asked Officer Daniels.

"Well, Amanda is, and I'm retired. Now I'm a private detective. The name's Doyle Malloy. I was working on the Wilde case, but obviously that's snowballed a bit here."

"Hold on," said Officer Daniels, taking out a walkie-talkie. "I'm in the woods behind the catering van. I've found Ms. Wong. She appears to be alive. Please send paramedics."

"Technically, we found her," said Doyle.

"Excuse me?" asked Officer Daniels.

"Well, on the walkie-talkie there, you said *you* found her. But *we* did."

"I think it's time for you folks to be runnin' along now. The police can handle it from here."

"We've already been working on this, and I don't—" began Amanda.

"I'm sorry. Mandy. Doodle. You guys gotta scram. We have a police matter. I think the Nisswa Police Department is well-equipped to handle this. Go back to Murderapolis."

"It's Amanda and Doyle, and we have critical information," said Amanda.

"I'm sure you do. If we need help, we'll contact you. It looks like my back-up has arrived."

Four more cops made their way through the crowd.

"Ambulance is comin'," said one of them.

"All right," said Officer Daniels. "I need everyone to BACK UP! BACK UP, I SAID! MOVE!"

As ordered, the gawkers flowed away like the ocean at low tide. The ambulance pulled up near the edge of the forest, next to the catering truck.

"William?"

"What'd you say?" Doyle asked Amanda.

"I didn't say anything," she said.

"William, is that you?"

"Oh, shit—she's awake," said Doyle.

"Load her on the stretcher," said Officer Daniels.

"Wait, wait, wait," said Doyle, running alongside the stretcher as the paramedics gave him nasty looks. "Eva, what happened in your trailer? Who hurt you?"

"I don't . . ."

"Think, Eva. You have to remember something," pleaded Doyle.

"I think that's just about enough, Doohickey. You can ask questions later. When we're done with our investigation." Officer Daniels slapped Doyle on the back and pulled him backwards, making way for the paramedics to load Eva into the ambulance.

"But . . ."

Amanda put an arm around Doyle. "It's okay—we'll ask her later. I don't think she'll be much help right now."

"William . . . ?" Eva asked no one in particular. The paramedics slammed the ambulance doors shut.

"Yeah, I guess so," said Doyle. "At least she'll probably be near William in the hospital. They'll both be happy."

19

Doyle and Amanda silently ate salads at Rafferty's in Nisswa. Doyle wasn't very happy with how things were going, and not just with the bland veggies he was munching on. The whole case stunk. They'd been making progress on Wilde's murder. The bite marks on his thighs, the provocative photos, the threatening note on their motel door, the kidnapping of Eva—all of it made it feel like they were getting close.

Now, with William's stabbing and Eva tossed into the woods, it felt like the whole Wilde case was getting sidetracked.

Doyle stopped eating. He was staring at the lettuce leaf at the end of his fork.

"Something wrong?" asked Amanda.

Doyle dropped the fork on to the table with a loud clank. "She faked it," he said.

"Who?"

"Eva. She faked the whole thing," he said, shaking his head.

"That's what I figured," said Amanda. "I was just waiting for you to come to that same conclusion."

"You were?" asked Doyle.

"She's an actress, but she's not that good an actress. All that 'William, are you there?' nonsense when she 'awoke' was just ridiculous."

"Why didn't you say anything?" asked Doyle.

"Well, when you slapped her, I assumed you already knew. I mean, that's a clever way to snap her out of her role. But now I realize that you had no clue, which suggests we really need to go over standard medical response procedures."

Doyle shrugged his shoulders. "Eh?"

"What finally clued you in?" asked Amanda.

"Well, the fact that there was blood all over her trailer, but no discernible injury on her body. For her to bleed that much, there'd have to be visible lacerations somewhere."

Amanda nodded.

"And all of this conveniently makes her look innocent," said Doyle.

"So you think she's guilty? You think she killed Wilde?"

"I do," said Doyle.

"If I had to take a guess, she probably staged her trailer incident first, drove to our hotel to post the note . . . somewhere in that time, she most likely called the police and reported a disturbance in one of the trailers in Nisswa Park. That would leave plenty of time for the police to investigate and set up a perimeter. Then, after they have it blocked off, she sneaks in through the woods, drops to the ground, and waits for someone to see her."

"Whose blood is in her trailer?" asked Amanda.

Doyle thought about it. "I really have no idea."

"Do you think she acted alone?"

"Could've. I still don't know why she would have killed Wilde, unless it was somehow related to the photographs, or simply a relationship gone horribly wrong."

"Do you think she stabbed William?"

Doyle shook his head. "No, that wouldn't make any sense. She wouldn't take the chance of being seen like that, especially when the police were conducting a search for her. Someone else did that."

"But who, and why?" asked Amanda. "Either it was a random stabbing, or someone was working with her."

"Or against her," said Doyle.

"That could be," said Amanda. "But if it's someone working with her, then we better get to the hospital."

"Why's that?"

"Because if Eva wants William dead, then she has the perfect opportunity right now. They're at the hospital together."

"Oh, shit."

"Indeed."

"Hey, that Mike Cameron is there, too, isn't he?"

"He is. Hopefully he'll be willing to talk to us, too. But first, we better make sure that William's okay."

Doyle nodded.

Amanda was about to stand up, but Doyle grabbed her hand. She sat back down.

"Yes?"

"Will you stick close to me? I can't imagine what I'd do if you got stabbed like William."

"That's very sweet, Doyle. Don't worry, I know how to protect myself. I'm a cop, you know. But I'll still stick close to you."

Doyle gently patted her hand. "Good. Thank you."

She smiled at him.

"All right, let's go save William's life from his ex-wife."

"Sounds like a plan," said Amanda.

Doyle threw a few bills onto the table and within seconds they were heading down the highway.

20

Well, well—look who decided to make a return appearance to our hospital. How's your stomach, Detective? Are you going to make a mess of any more of our patients?"

Doyle lowered his head and coughed. "Listen, Nurse Gina . . . I'm sorry about that mishap the other night."

"Mishap? You threw up all over the corpse of Davis Wilde! That's not a mishap, Detective. That's atrocious. Not to mention disgusting. I can't believe—"

"Yes, well, sorry about that. Can you tell me where William Wright is located?"

"Are you planning on throwing up on him?"

Doyle grimaced. "No. No, I'm not."

"Then follow me."

Amanda looked at Doyle and bit back laughter. Doyle rolled his eyes.

As they walked down the hall, Doyle asked Gina, "Do you happen to know where Eva Wong is currently located?"

"Yes, she's in the same room as Mr. Wright."

"What? Why?"

"Because there are not many rooms, quite frankly."

"But they're the opposite sex. And they used to be married."

Gina looked down at her clipboard. "Really?"

"But they got divorced," said Amanda. "They tend to get somewhat violent whenever they're close to each other."

"Well," said Gina. "That would have been good information to have. The policemen who brought her in didn't tell me a thing."

"No surprise there," said Doyle.

"The room is right down here," said Gina, walking a little faster. "Right here, in fact."

Gina opened the door, revealing William and Eva engaged in a passionate kiss.

"Well I'll be damned," said Gina. "They appear to be doin' pretty good for ex-spouses."

William broke off the kiss when he realized they had an audience.

"Ah, Doyle," he said. "Look—I found Eva!"

"Yeah, so did we awhile ago. How are you doing, William?"

"A little sore, I suppose. Emotionally I'm doing quite well, though."

Amanda walked over to Eva.

"How are you holding up?"

Eva stretched out her shoulders and rubbed her head. "I'm also rather sore. I can't remember much of anything today. Do you have any idea how I ended up in those woods?"

Doyle and Amanda looked at each other. "No idea," said Doyle. "Someone must have given you a pretty hard bump to the noggin for you to lose your memory like that."

"Maybe," said Eva. "I mean, my head feels a little woozy. Not too bad though. Just . . . my whole body kind of hurts."

"I'm just so happy that she's okay," said William.

"We're happy that both of you are safe," said Amanda.

"Yes, and in the same room," said Doyle. "That's fantastic."

"Isn't that just the strangest coincidence?" asked William. Eva hugged him.

Doyle sighed. "You know what? I really don't like hospitals. I think I'm going to get some air."

"Maybe I'll join you," said Amanda. "I could use some fresh air myself."

"We'll be right back," said Doyle.

STANDING IN THE DESIGNATED SMOKING AREA twenty-five yards from the hospital door, Doyle asked Amanda, "What the hell is going on in there? The fact that Eva is probably behind all this scares the bejeezus out of me. The way she's acting . . . ugh."

"At least no one's dead. I don't think she'd do anything now, because it'd be pretty darned obvious who did it."

"So . . . what do you think?"

"We should talk to Mike Cameron. Let's find out what he knows."

GINA POINTED AT THE DOOR. "Here's Mike Cameron's room. Hopefully he's not kissing anybody."

Gina knocked first, waited a few seconds, then turned the handle and pushed the door open.

"Looks fine to me," said Gina. "Have fun."

"Thanks," said Doyle.

The room looked the same as William and Eva's room, except that this one was packed to the brim with flowers, balloons, and other gifts that read, "Get Well Soon!"

Mike Cameron was asleep, his head covered in bandages.

"Mr. Cameron?" said Doyle.

No response.

"Mr. Cameron?" he repeated.

Still no response.

Doyle kicked the bedframe. The entire bed shook. Mike Cameron jerked awake, eyes wide.

"Who's that? What's happening? Who are you?"

"Mike Cameron? My name is Detective Doyle Malloy, and this is Amanda Hutchins, MPD. We're here investigating the death of Davis Wilde."

Cameron groaned. "Aww, this again? I've already been over and over this with the police. I already told them I don't know anything else! Can't you just let me rest?"

"Maybe later, Mr. Cameron," said Doyle. "For now, we just need to hear it again, firsthand. This could prove to be very important."

Cameron sighed. "Fine. Okay. What do you want to know?"

"Let's start at the beginning," said Doyle. "You were shooting a scene for *Fargo II*, is that right?"

"The deuce. Correct," said Cameron.

"What was the mood on the set?"

"Tense," Cameron said. "Ms. Coen had done a substantial amount of yelling, which wasn't uncommon, but it was beginning to wear on people's nerves."

"What was she yelling about?" asked Amanda.

"The usual stuff. No one could do their job right. That sort of thing."

"Was she yelling at anyone in particular?" asked Amanda.

"It seems to me now that she was yelling mostly at Wilde, but that could just be my mind playing tricks on me."

"What happened?" asked Amanda.

"You know that already, don't you?"

"We do, but we want to hear it from you," she said.

"All right, well—we were doing a scene in which my character shoots his character. They had everything rigged for the special effects. I was supposed to pull the trigger and yank the gun, which would make the fake blood burst out of Wilde's prosthetic face."

"But?"

"It wasn't fake blood," said Cameron, looking down at his right hand. "When the gun went off, I didn't realize what had happened at first. I thought it sounded awfully loud for a blank. Then again, I really haven't shot much of anything, blanks or no."

"What happened after you shot—" Doyle stopped himself and decided to carefully rearrange his words. "What happened after the shot went off?"

"Within seconds I realized what happened. And within those seconds, I felt this wave of horror. I collapsed. I don't remember anything after that."

"Nothing at all?"

"No. I found out later that I hit my head pretty hard. I don't think I need to still be in the hospital, but Mr. Winthrop says I need to. Apparently it's better for insurance purposes if I stay here."

Doyle made a mental note of that comment.

"Like I said, I really don't know much more than that," said Cameron. "I wish I did know who did it. I first suspected Chip, since he does all the effects and stuff, but I can't think of any reason *why* he would. You know?"

"I understand," said Doyle. "You sure have a lot of flowers and gifts. Who are all these from? Fans?"

"I don't have too many fans," said Cameron. "I'm mostly a stage actor, so I don't have a ton of paparazzi following me around. This stuff is mostly from my family and friends."

"Where are you from, Mike?"

"Edina."

That explains it, thought Doyle. *Rich yuppie.*

"Thank you for all your help, Mike. We really appreciate it."

Doyle and Amanda turned to leave when Cameron called out to them.

"Hey, guys—do you know what's happening with the film? They're not still shooting are they?"

"I don't think so," said Amanda.

"Oh, good," said Cameron. "I just want to make sure they don't start without me."

"That probably won't happen," said Doyle. "Unless they find an actor who looks just like you."

The thought of this seemed to truly frighten Mike Cameron.

"Have a nice evening," Doyle said, then left with Amanda.

21

here are we going?" asked Amanda.

"Back to Nisswa Park. I have some interviewing I want to do," said Doyle, applying some extra pressure to the gas pedal.

"But what about William and Eva?"

Doyle gently patted her leg. "I think you're right. I don't think Eva will try anything tonight. It'd be far too obvious. In fact, *not* doing anything will add to her defense. That'd be the smart play."

"So, who are we going to interview?"

"Our current employer, Mr. Winthrop. Just because he's paying for our services doesn't mean he couldn't be guilty in some way himself."

"Are you having certain suspicions?"

"Nothing in particular, mind you," said Doyle. "It's just that Mike Cameron mentioned something about insurance, and that got me to thinking that all of what's transpired might be well above love triangles and petty scorn. Maybe it's all business."

"You think Wilde may have been killed for insurance money? That's quite a stretch," said Amanda.

"Maybe so, but it can't hurt to pursue that avenue."

Amanda nodded. "Fair enough. You know, I get more impressed with you by the hour."

Doyle looked at her, cocked his eyebrow, and said, "That's what all the ladies tell me."

"CAR!" Amanda yelled.

Doyle swerved, narrowly missing an on-coming Volkswagen.

"Just keep your eyes on the road, Casanova. I'll be most impressed with you if we solve this case without dying in the process."

"That's good enough for me," said Doyle.

"THIS IS WINTHROP'S PLACE, RIGHT?" asked Doyle.

"Yup, this is the one," said Amanda.

Doyle knocked on the thin, metal door. A tall, blonde figure with excessive make-up greeted them.

"Oh, I'm sorry ma'am," said Doyle. "We're looking for the producer, Mr. Winthrop."

"Doyle . . ." Amanda said. She elbowed Doyle.

"Well, I—" the blonde began.

Doyle interrupted. "Is he here? Is he out for the evening? Are you his girlfriend?"

"No, but—"

"You certainly can't be his wife. After all, you're far too attractive for that. Am I right?"

"Doyle, you should stop," said Amanda, laughing uneasily.

Doyle put his arm around the blonde. "Please, miss. Can you tell us where Mr. Winthrop is?"

"Hands off, Bub," said the blonde in a shockingly deep voice.

Doyle took a step back.

"This is sort of a hobby for me," said Winthrop, removing his wig.

"It's been a long couple days here," said Doyle. "And I wasn't expecting you to look quite so, umm . . ."

Amanda and Winthrop both looked at Doyle expectantly.

"You know what? Never mind," said Doyle. "Let's move on."

"That would be great," said Amanda.

"C'mon in," said Winthrop. "Take a seat on my couch. It's small, but it works."

"What should we do with these?" asked Doyle, holding up a pile of wigs that lay strewn across the cushions.

"Oh, just throw those onto the vanity over there, next to the others," said Winthrop.

"Okie dokie," said Doyle.

"Well, have you solved the crime? Did you catch Wilde's killer so I can start up my movie again?"

"I think we're close," said Doyle. "We have a few questions that we really have to ask before we proceed with the investigation."

"Fair enough," said Winthrop. "What sort of questions do you have?"

"First of all, insurance," said Doyle. "Did you have insurance on Wilde?"

Winthrop nodded and answered without hesitation. "I know where you're going with this, and the answer is yes, we do carry insurance on all of our actors and crew. It's standard industry practice. Frankly, we'll get from the insurance company roughly what we paid Wilde for his contract, plus an additional sum to find a replacement."

"Are you expecting the replacement actor to be more or less expensive than Wilde?" asked Doyle.

Winthrop coughed. "This is to remain in the room, but I've found a replacement actor, and he will indeed be more expensive than Wilde."

"How much more expensive?" asked Amanda.

"Substantially," said Winthrop. "I had to find someone who looked fairly close to Wilde, and would be accessible within a day's notice, once the murder investigation has wrapped up."

"Who'd you find?" asked Doyle.

"Josh Hartnett," said Winthrop.

Doyle shrugged. "He looks a little bit like Wilde, I guess."

"Close enough," said Winthrop. "We got lucky. He was visiting family in Brainerd, and I was able to convince him that playing Wilde's role would be a beautiful tribute and a smart PR move. Of course, he's a big star, and, therefore, not cheap. We'll do some CGI work and make him look exactly like Wilde. That'll be another added cost. This damn movie is getting really expensive." He shook his head.

"As you know, Mr. Winthrop, there's also been a stabbing on set. My partner, in fact."

Winthrop looked at Amanda. "She looks great, considering."

"Not her," said Doyle. "William. The British guy."

"Oh," said Winthrop. "Ooohhh."

"No, not like that," said Doyle. "William's cute, but he's my business partner. Amanda here is my other partner . . . for that."

"Doyle!" exclaimed Amanda.

"Okay, never mind again," said Doyle. "Also, there was an assault, of sorts, involving Eva Wong."

"I heard. The police haven't given me all the details on that yet. Is she okay?" asked Winthrop.

Doyle looked at Amanda, trying to gauge how much information he should give to Winthrop.

"She'll be okay," said Doyle. "She was unconscious for a while, and there was a lot of blood in her trailer, but at this point it doesn't appear that it was hers."

"That's odd," said Winthrop.

"Quite," said Doyle. "We're still working on that, too. We'll give you details when we can."

"Am I paying extra for that?" asked Winthrop.

"Since it feeds into the case we're working on now, we'll consider it to be part of our daily expenses."

"Terrific," said Winthrop.

"A fifteen-percent gratuity may be added, however," said Doyle.

"That's about the strangest thing I've ever heard," said Winthrop.

"Well, we're strange detectives," said Doyle. Amanda rolled her eyes.

"Clearly. Anything else, detectives?"

Doyle shook his head, but Amanda stood up.

"Mr. Winthrop," she said. "Does this couch turn into a bed, by any chance?"

"It does. Why do you ask?"

Doyle immediately realized what Amanda was getting at. "You lead a fairly active social life, do you not?" asked Doyle.

"What does that even mean?" asked Winthrop.

Doyle coughed. "Did you have a nasty, sweaty orgy on this bed a few nights ago?"

"Good Lord, you couldn't be a little more subtle?" Amanda asked.

"I tried that, but he didn't pick up on it," said Doyle.

Winthrop held up a hand.

"I did, indeed. How did you know?" asked Winthrop.

"Chip took some photos," said Amanda. "We're not positive, but it sounds like Maura Coen may have put him up to it."

"Maura? But why?"

"We don't have all the answers yet, but we'll get them," said Amanda.

Winthrop nodded. "I see."

"Is there anything that happened during that evening of . . . *socializing* that might be of importance?" asked Amanda.

"I don't think so," said Winthrop. "Listen, this is very important to me. If you have any specific questions, I'll answer them. But I don't much care for discussing my personal life, and I especially don't want it going anywhere beyond our small group here."

"Did you bite Wilde?" asked Doyle.

"Pardon?" responded Winthrop.

"Did you bite Wilde on his thigh?"

Winthrop thought about it for a moment. "I haven't bitten anyone in years. I'm not the rough type."

"Did you see anyone bite him?" asked Doyle.

"No, I didn't. Honestly, it was a very pleasant evening."

"Did you get the feeling that any sort of jealousy was flaring up between the four of you?" asked Doyle.

"Three of you," said Winthrop.

"Three?" asked Doyle.

"Yes, it was Davis Wilde, Tina, and me. Who else claims they were there?" asked Winthrop, appearing truly confused.

"The photos very clearly show Eva Wong," said Doyle.

"Do you have them with?" asked Amanda.

"I do," he said, digging into his coat pocket.

"This whole concept is preposterous," said Winthrop.

"Why?" asked Amanda.

"Eva Wong had no interest speaking with anyone on set, let alone having sex with them. If the photos show her in here, then they were definitely doctored on that PhotoShack or whatever they call it."

"Mr. Winthrop," said Doyle. "Are you trying to tell me that this is not definitive proof?"

Doyle held up one particular snapshot of the orgy. The one that showed a brunette watching intently from somewhere within the trailer. Her hair and part of her face was visible.

"Ha!" bellowed Winthrop.

"What? What's so funny?" asked Doyle.

Amanda got it before Doyle.

"Look where the windows are," she said. "The bed is here, which means the photographer was behind that window, next to the vanity."

Doyle looked toward where Amanda was pointing. Then he looked at the photograph. Then he looked back towards the window.

"Oh, for fuck's sake," said Doyle. "It's not Eva Wong in the photo. It's a wig on a mannequin head."

Once again, Ronald Winthrop cackled with laughter.

"I can't even remember what I'm paying you, but I'm positive it's too much," Winthrop said.

"You have to admit, it closely resembles Eva Wong," said Doyle.

"Absolutely, if she were an inanimate object," Winthrop said, holding his chest, attempting to subdue the laughter.

"You know, this is rather interesting," said Amanda. "Maura Coen was positive that Eva Wong was responsible for the murder, and she actually handed us these photographs as if they were proof supporting that theory. Did she really have any idea if Eva was in the trailer or not? Or did she just see the photos, saw what she thought was Eva, and try to pin the blame on her?"

"But why?" asked Doyle.

"Allow me to offer a little insight into the minds of both of these women," said Winthrop. "Eva Wong I've only known for a short time. What I can tell you is that she is extremely professional, although not terribly social. She did in fact have an attraction for Davis Wilde, which anyone with eyes could easily notice. Same with Maura. However, one thing I can tell you positively about Maura Coen is that once you cross her, you can never make it up to her."

"What exactly do you mean by that?" asked Amanda.

"I've known Maura for several years. I actually met her while she was a film student at NYU, well after her brothers had already made a name for themselves. We met at a party on campus. She was speaking at great length as to why she was Jean-Luc Goddard's biggest fan. Naturally, I had to refute her argument by claiming that I was indeed Jean-Luc Goddard's biggest fan. Truth be told, neither of us liked Goddard's work, but it was NYU, and one doesn't get ahead in NYU without extreme pretentiousness. Should the director's name ever arise in conversation, she will give me such a fierce glare that the devil himself would wet his trousers."

"That's quite the image," said Doyle.

"So do you think she could have done this?" asked Amanda. "Out of jealousy for Wilde? She didn't want Eva to have him, so she took him out?"

"I really doubt it," said Winthrop. "While she does carry incredible grudges, and can be vicious as a Doberman, I can assure you that this film is far more important to her than any physical attraction. I'd say the number one goal in her life is to make a more successful film than her brothers. Obviously a murder on the film set would jeopardize that goal. I don't think she'd risk it."

"Could she possibly think that *Fargo II* would be more successful than the original?" asked Doyle.

"Stranger things have happened," said Winthrop. "At any rate, it's worth trying."

"We should get going," said Doyle. "I want to get back to William."

Amanda nodded. "Thank you, Mr. Winthrop. We'll go through our information and get this case solved. The sooner we do that, the faster your filming can commence."

Winthrop wiped some sweat from his brow, accidentally taking some foundation with it. "Absolutely. Really, if any other questions come up, don't hesitate to ask me. Stop by any time."

22

William's head was in a cloud. A big, fluffy cloud. Although he knew that wasn't quite right.

He was in a room of some sort. What kind of room? He was pretty sure it was a white one.

What was he doing there?

William vaguely recalled the sharp pain in his side, although it seemed as if it were centuries ago.

He opened his eyes, but the light was overwhelming, so he snapped them shut again.

Someone was with him. He couldn't see who it was, but there was definitely someone there. Not that he was concerned. It was merely a bemused awareness.

He felt himself fading again. Retreating from the clouds back into the darker area.

It was moments, or maybe hours later when some loud noises pulled him away from a deep slumber. He couldn't make out anything in particular. Just a lot of movement. Did someone open the door?

Someone must have, or how else did a wasp get in the room? The one that settled on his neck. Then stung him. And kept stinging him.

WILLIAM WAS NO LONGER ASLEEP. Quite the opposite. Everything had gone haywire.

23

hat exactly are we doing, Doyle?"

"We're driving to the hospital," he said, adjusting the rear-view mirror.

"What's the plan?" asked Amanda.

Doyle cleared his throat. "Okay," he said. "Here's what's going down. We're going to pull into the hospital. We're going to march right up to William's room. Then we're going to yank him out of his bed. Then we're going to place him right in the back seat here. Then we're going to drive away."

"What about Eva?"

"Irrelevant," said Doyle. "Whether she's present in the room, or whether she's a homicidal maniac, it really doesn't matter. Either way, I'm taking William with us. Assuming he's alive and well."

"I'm sure he's fine," said Amanda. "Like you said before, I really doubt Eva would try anything while they're in the room together. It'd be too obvious."

"Still, the idea of William being absolutely vulnerable gives me the willies. We really shouldn't have left him alone, even if logic was on our side," said Doyle.

"That may be so. But you do realize that, with a knife wound, they're not going to take too kindly to us abducting him."

"That Nurse Gina had a strong personality, but I'm sure I could take her down if worse came to worse," said Doyle.

"That's sweet, Doyle—but you couldn't take down a one-legged ballet dancer," said Amanda with a smile, nudging Doyle in his side.

"Ouch," said Doyle. "That's quite the burn, Ms. Hutchins. You know I'll be serving that right back to you soon enough."

"Bring it on, Malloy. Hey, you almost missed our exit," she said.

Doyle drove along the frontage road, then into the hospital parking lot.

"Why do we keep ending up here?" asked Doyle.

"Well, people keep getting hurt," said Amanda.

"Let's try to stop anything further from happening. I'm kind of getting sick of the Nisswa Municipal Hospital."

"Amen to that," said Amanda.

"WHICH WAY IS IT AGAIN?" DOYLE ASKED AMANDA.

"Not that way," said Amanda. "Mike Cameron's room is down that hall. Here, come this way," she said.

Doyle followed down the familiar looking hall. He felt a chill. It dawned on him how strangely quiet it was. Except for the whirring of a few machines, the hospital was quiet.

Dead quiet, thought Doyle.

Stopping in front of one of the rooms, Amanda said, "Here we go. Let's hope for the best."

As she turned the knob and pushed the door open, it became clear things were not how they should be.

Eva's bed was empty. When Doyle pulled back the curtain separating William's bed from Eva's, that's when he panicked.

William was convulsing. Foam dripped down his cheeks, plopping onto the linoleum floor next to the bed. His eyes were rolled back in his head. A syringe was sticking out of his neck.

"Get the nurse, get the nurse, get the nurse," Doyle hollered, but Amanda was already exiting the room with her gun drawn.

"Oh, what the hell is happening," said Doyle, pulling the syringe out of William's neck. A single drop of blood surfaced, which quickly dissipated into the slick, sweaty surface of William's skin.

A nurse Doyle didn't recognize charged into the room moments later, although it felt like hours to Doyle.

"My God," said the nurse. Doyle saw that her name was Carolyn. "What'd he do?"

Doyle held up the syringe.

"This was sticking out of his neck," he said.

"His heart rate is off the charts," she said, looking at the monitor. "I'll be right back with a sedative."

Within seconds, the nurse was back in the room, tapping on a small, plastic syringe with a very long needle.

"What are you going to do with that?" asked Doyle.

"This needle is going into his heart. If his heart keeps pumping like it is right now, it's going to stop, or maybe explode."

"This is just like *Pulp Fiction*," said Doyle.

"Just hold him down!"

Doyle did as he was told and held William down by the shoulders. His eyes were still rolling in the back of his head, the rest of his body still jerking and convulsing.

"Be careful," said Doyle. "He's English."

Nurse Carolyn gave him a confused look, but was still very focused on the task at hand.

"Should I count to three?" asked Doyle.

"Sure," said the nurse.

"One . . . two . . ."

Nurse Carolyn stabbed the needle into William's chest before Doyle could finish the countdown.

As the nurse pushed the plunger, the effects became apparent right away. The incessant beeping coming from the heart monitor slowed down considerably. While William was still twitching, the movements were becoming less grandiose. Instead of his eyes rolling back, they simply remained closed.

"Is he okay? Is he going to be okay?" asked Doyle.

"Too soon to tell," said Nurse Carolyn. "Right now, he's stabilizing. I'll need to monitor him carefully for the next couple hours. Which one of you did it?"

"Did what?" asked Doyle.

The nurse held up the syringe that had been in William's neck.

"Who gave him drugs?" asked the nurse.

"Oh, that was there when we got here," he said.

"Uh-huh," she said, obviously not believing a word of it.

"What was he drugged with?" asked Doyle.

"I can't say yet without further testing," she said. "But definitely uppers of some sort. Probably cocaine."

"Cocaine?" asked Doyle. "Are you sure it's not some drug the hospital carries?"

"I doubt it," she said.

"How can you be so sure?" asked Doyle.

"The syringe. We don't use any like that in this hospital. That thing looks like it came from the eighties."

Doyle thought for a moment. "The woman who was in here, on that bed, was his ex-wife. She may have tried to murder him. Do you know where she went?"

"I really don't know," the nurse said.

"Do you have cameras anywhere in this room? How about in the hallway?"

"Honey," said the nurse, "We don't have any cameras in this hospital. You're in Nisswa, Minnesota. We're not exactly rolling in the dough."

"That's not the first time I've heard that," said Doyle.

"Now, I have to ask you to leave. Let me work," said the nurse.

Doyle nodded. "Okay."

Footsteps echoed down the hallway until Amanda came into the room. "Doyle!" said Amanda, putting her gun back in her holster. "I couldn't find her anywhere. Is William okay?"

Doyle nodded. "Right now he is. It wasn't looking too good, though. I think I just about had a heart attack."

"So did he," said the nurse, motioning her head towards William. "Will you both leave the room, please?"

"What now?" asked Amanda.

"Stay here with William. Wait outside the door," said Doyle. "If Eva comes back, shoot her."

"Okay, sounds like a plan," said Amanda. "What are you going to do?"

"As much as I hate saying it," said Doyle. "I'm going to contact the Nisswa police. We're going to need their help on this one. Either Eva's trying to make a break for it, or she's about to go on a bloody killing spree. No matter what happens, the police need to know what's going on. There's strength in numbers."

Amanda agreed. "Do it," she said. "But where are you going?"

"I'm going back to the film set," said Doyle. "I'm not sure why, exactly. Just a hunch. Eva's an attention seeker. If that's what this is all about, then that's the best place for her to go. Therefore, that's where I should go."

"Just come back safe. And call me immediately if anything goes wrong. Actually, call me even if things don't go wrong. I want to know what you're doing and what I can do to help."

"Really, the best help right now is just to keep William safe. I feel like an idiot that I even let him get into this situation."

"Don't beat yourself up. Just find her and stop her," said Amanda.

"See you soon," said Doyle.

With that, Doyle gave Amanda their briefest and best kiss to date.

24

Doyle drove down the highway, trying his best to punch numbers into his cell phone and keep his eyes on the road at the same time.

"Thank you for calling the Nisswa Police Department. How are you today?"

"Well, I guess I'm doing pretty—"

Before Doyle could fully respond, the voice said, "If you are calling from a touch-tone phone, please press one. If you are calling from a rotary phone, please hold."

A rotary phone? thought Doyle. *Do they still have those up here? WTF?*

"If someone you know is dead or may be dying, please press one now. If you are dead or may be dying, please press two now. If someone keyed your car, please press three now. If someone—"

Doyle pressed one and decided to keep the multitude of criticisms to himself. There was far too much to comment on. After answering a number of additional prompts and speaking briefly with a dispatcher, Doyle finally seemed to be getting somewhere.

"Officer Daniels," said the voice at the other end of the line.

Doyle hesitated.

"Are you . . . real?" he asked.

The voice sighed. "Yes, I'm real."

"You're . . . a living person?"

"Yes, yes, yes—I'm alive. Now what do you want?"

"This is Detective Doyle Malloy. If I'm not mistaken, we spoke earlier today in Nisswa Park. You called me Doodle."

"Oh, yeah . . . Doodle! How's that lady detective you were with? Merta? Was that her name?"

"Amanda. She's fine. But listen, I need your help. I think I may be able to help you."

"Uh-huh. Yeah. I'm sure," said Officer Daniels.

"Listen, the guy who was stabbed this morning. He's my partner. His name's William Wright," said Doyle.

"You guys fags or something?"

Doyle took the phone from his ear and rolled his eyes. He suddenly had an incredible urge to return to the Cities. He considered simply hanging up, but knew the tasks at hand were far too important.

"No, he's my business partner," said Doyle. "Someone tried to kill him again, and we know who did it."

"Oh, yeah? Who's that?" asked Officer Daniels.

"Eva Wong," said Doyle.

"Eva Wong? The actress?"

"That's right," said Doyle. "Remember, it seemed like she was unconscious this morning, but yet there were no visible signs of bruising on her head?"

Doyle heard silence on the other end.

He was about to say "Hello?" when Officer Daniels spoke again.

"Where are you, Doodle?"

"I'm heading down 371 towards the Nisswa Park. Why?"

"Just turn on County 77. There's a bar there called Kelly's. That's where most of us cops hang out."

"After your shifts end, of course," said Doyle.

"Yeah, right. Get there as soon as you can. I think we can share some information."

"Great," said Doyle. He heard a click, and then a dial tone.

Doyle wondered if he'd been better off on his own.

25

Kelly's Saloon in Nisswa wasn't all that different from the Martiniapolis, Doyle's usual hang-out, except for fact that Kelly's had an inordinate amount of sawdust on the floor, probably to cover the equally inordinate scent of urine.

Doyle looked at his wristband, the one his father gave him many years ago when Doyle was just a rookie. Etched into the band was *WWCD?* which served as a constant reminder to Doyle to be responsible, to question his decisions, to be a thorough detective.

Doyle looked around the tavern and thought to himself, what *would* Columbo do?

Based on the sketchy nature of the joint, Doyle assumed Columbo would try to get his information, then get out as fast as possible. And he'd probably do some squinting, too. Columbo was good at that.

A large, weather-beaten woman behind the bar asked Doyle, "Lost, are ya?"

Doyle shook his head. "I don't think so. I'm looking for someone."

The bartender pointed towards the back of the establishment. "Right back there. I take it you're lookin' for Gus?"

"Is his last name Daniels?"

"Of course," said the bartender. "He's our city's finest."

"Finest cop?" asked Doyle.

"No, finest drinker," said the bartender. Although I reckon he does some police work every now and again."

"Excellent," said Doyle. "Thank you."

The wood floors creaked as he walked past a few dart machines and, to his surprise, a cigarette vending machine. *I haven't seen one of those since the eighties*, he thought.

Officer Gus Daniels was sitting in the booth furthest to the back.

"Doodle!"

Doyle felt a wave of anger rush into him. He really loathed this guy, and he truly wondered if he was doing any good by speaking to him.

"Hi, Gus," said Doyle, sitting down across from the Nisswa policeman.

"Watch it," said the cop. "It's Officer Daniels. I'm not your boyfriend. Don't call me Gus. Got it?"

Doyle stood up. "If this isn't going to be productive, then I really need to go. A murderer is on the loose. I'm not going to waste my valuable time bullshitting with a drunk cop."

"Sit down, Doyle."

The fact that Officer Daniels used Doyle's real name perked his interest and made him hesitate.

"You didn't call me Doodle," he said.

"I know your name," said Daniels. "I was just fuckin' with ya. C'mon, don't take it so hard."

"Alright, fine. What is it you wanted me to know?"

"Well, it's not quite that simple," said Daniels.

Doyle sighed. *Of course not. It never is.*

"You're looking for a little quid pro-quo, is that it?" asked Doyle.

Daniels stared at Doyle blankly. "What the fuck are you talking about?" he asked.

Doyle found himself wanting a drink, but decided against it. "You have information for me, but you won't give it unless I give you something in return."

"Yeah, that's right," said Officer Daniels. "I thought you were trying to give me sushi or somethin'."

Doyle faked a laugh. "That sure would be a wacky turn in the conversation. No—I simply want to know what information you have for me. I'm all ears."

"Okay," said Daniels, stubbing out his cigarette. "But here's the deal. If I tell you what I know, then you can't take the credit if you catch her."

"Come again?" asked Doyle. "You're saying that, no matter what, you're taking the credit for catching the killer?"

Daniels appeared to think about it momentarily. "Yeah, that's the gist of it."

"Well, why should I bother doing anything, then? If you're just going to take the credit, you might as well get out there and do your job. I can just head back to the Cities."

Daniels shook his head. "I don't think so," he said.

"Why not?"

"Your partner got stabbed, and his ex-wife is likely the assailant as well as Wilde's murderer. You're personally involved. Therefore, it's your mess. You clean it up."

The succinctness of the speech hit Doyle hard. For better or worse, it was absolutely a mess, and it was all Doyle's.

"You seem to be pretty sure Eva Wong is responsible for everything. Other than what I just told you on the phone about her attempt to kill William at the hospital, what makes you think she also murdered Wilde?"

Daniels took a gulp of what looked like a cranberry vodka. Heavy on the vodka, light on the cranberry.

"She's nuts," said Daniels. "She stabbed a guy, faked a kidnapping, then tried to kill him again. That's nuts."

"Maybe, but that was all concerning her ex-husband. I can't say one way or another what their relationship was like, but needless to say, they had a history together. It certainly can't be used as evidence in the murder of Davis Wilde," said Doyle.

"There's more to it than that," said Daniels. "The little scene in her trailer? She made a big mistake. To make it look like a scuffle had taken place, she used fake blood. The same consistency as the blood found in the prop trailer. The same trailer that holds the blank rounds. Is this making some sense to you?"

"It means she's been in the prop trailer at least once. Still not solid evidence," said Doyle.

Daniels cleared his throat. "Oh yeah? Well, try this on for size. We found a bite mark on Wilde's thigh. It matches a bite mark taken off an apple in Eva Wong's trailer. We also found a substantial amount of vomit on Wilde's body after it was brought to the hospital. We still haven't matched it up to anyone. Very strange."

It was Doyle's turn to clear his throat. "Yes, that is quite strange. Peculiar, really. But even if Eva had bitten Wilde on the thigh, that's still very circumstantial. If you believe the tabloids, then you'll know that many, many people have slept with him."

"But not all of them had been in the prop trailer," said Daniels.

Doyle nodded.

"Thank you, Officer Daniels," said Doyle. "Actually, this conversation has been surprising helpful."

"Please, call me Gus."

"But you said—"

"Go get the killer, Doodle. Do whatever it takes. Just make sure when you're done, you let everyone know that Officer Gus Daniels figured it out."

"What are you going to do in the meantime?" asked Doyle.

"You're looking at it," said Daniels. "Oh, and I'll put out an APB, so all the cops in the area will be looking for Eva Wong."

"Just not you," said Doyle.

"Get out of here, smart-ass," said Daniels. He polished off the last of his light pink beverage.

"Are you leaving? You know, you just had an alcoholic beverage while on duty. Not only is that against police code, but you're also putting others at risk."

Daniels looked at Doyle as if he were a space alien.

"Jesus, I had a drink. It's not like I just smoked a pound of crack. Don't be such a pussy."

"Fair enough," said Doyle.

"Really, please, leave. I can't wait for you to get out of my city. You bother me," said Daniels.

"Toodles," said Doyle. He saw a look of disgust on Daniels's face in his peripheral vision as he turned towards the exit.

As Doyle got into his car, he once again looked at his wristband.

What would Columbo do?

Doyle couldn't think of an episode in which Columbo had been called a pussy. As he started the ignition, Doyle thought to himself, *I guess I have to make the rest up as I go.*

"Hey, Honey Bunny," Doyle said into his cell phone. "How's everything at the hospital?"

"Settled down," said Amanda. "I haven't seen Eva anywhere. Then again, I haven't left the room much. I'm scared if I leave William alone for even a minute, something will happen, and I'll be responsible."

"You don't need to think like that. But thank you for watching over him. Really," said Doyle.

"What are you doing right now?" she asked.

"Driving back to the hotel. I had no idea it'd gotten so late. I'm going to get a couple hours of sleep. If Eva's decided to flee, it won't matter too much. I just talked to Officer Daniels, and he's sending out an APB. Hopefully someone will find her."

"If she hasn't fled completely, I have a pretty good idea of where she'll show up tomorrow," said Amanda.

"Oh, yeah?"

"It seems Eva was in such a hurry, she forgot to unplug her cell phone that was charging on the nurse's table."

Doyle laughed. "Really? What info were you able to get from it?"

"Nothing too substantial. The calls in and out were minimal, and only a few texts were still in her inbox. But the text of interest was just sent a few hours ago by Winthrop. He plans on resuming filming tomorrow morning, with whatever cast and crew they have available."

"Was the text sent specifically to Eva?"

"I can't really tell. The way it's worded, I assume it was sent to everyone involved with the film, not just her."

"Hmm," said Doyle. "Well, it's good to know. But still—do you really think she'd show up on set, just to get arrested?"

"Possibly," said Amanda. "If she's on a serious crime spree, maybe she really wants to go down in a blaze of glory."

"Could be," said Doyle. "I guess we'll just have to wait and see."

"I guess," she said.

"Are you going to be okay there tonight? You know—without me?"

"Well, I do have another brilliant, attractive detective in the room with me, so I'll probably be okay."

"He's unconscious, right?" asked Doyle.

"Yeah, he is," she said.

"Good," said Doyle.

"I doubt I'll be able to sleep, but that's probably for the best. I'd rather remain vigilant," Amanda said. "In fact, I looked out the door here, and a couple cops just came in. I'll have them do a thorough search of the hospital, just in case Eva's hiding out somewhere here and planning another attempt at William's life."

"Good idea," said Doyle. "If you have any trouble at all, call me."

"I will," she said. "All right, I should go. I want talk to these guys. Besides, I don't have very good reception in here. I'm getting a lot of static on this end."

"Okay, that's fine. Hey, Amanda?"

"Yes, Doyle?"

Doyle hesitated. He'd wanted to say something for a while now, and with how dangerous things had gotten, it seemed like now was the appropriate time. Still, he was suddenly, awfully nervous.

Here goes nothing, he thought.

"I love you," he said.

"What was that?" she said. "Sorry, you're breaking up."

"Olive juice," he said. "I had a martini and got olive juice all over me. It was really weird. I gotta go."

"Doyle?" he heard Amanda say again as he hung up.

"Dammit," Doyle said, and pulled into the hotel parking lot. That was not how he'd intended the conversation to go.

Now that he was off the phone and sitting in the dark lot, he realized how quiet it was. Doyle looked at his watch. It was nearly three o'clock in the morning. As he got out of his car, every sound he made seemed to echo.

He thought of Eva Wong, who attempted to kill William not once but twice, and now it was looking like she even killed Wilde over a romance gone sour. A murderer on the loose. She probably thought she'd successfully killed William. Who would she go after next? Obviously it would be Doyle. After all, he was the other lead detective on the case.

Doyle bit his lip.

He tip-toed the few yards across the parking lot, all the while looking over his shoulder for any signs of movement. Once he got to the hotel door, he opened it quickly and leaped inside.

Doyle was relieved to find that there was no gun pointing at him when he got inside, nor a knife to his neck or throat. As Officer Daniels had so kindly pointed out, Doyle was a pussy. He knew it to be true, but didn't care. Now that he had someone he loved in his life, he felt as though he had something to lose. He had to be careful.

As he crawled into his empty bed, in his empty room, he thought of Amanda and longed to be with her.

But he knew what had to happen first. Tomorrow, he was quite certain, was going to be a very important day.

27

Doyle awoke to a knock on the door. He pulled himself out of bed and almost made it to the door before realizing he was wearing only his underwear. If it was Amanda, who he presumed it was, he wouldn't really care. However, he'd gotten into some trouble during his last case when a suspect showed up in the middle of the night. Doyle decided from that point on he wouldn't allow suspects to see his . . . fragility.

Tugging on a pair of pajama bottoms, Doyle scurried to the door and looked out the peephole. Doyle's jaw just about dropped to the ground when he saw that it was William. Doyle yanked the door open.

"William!" he yelled enthusiastically. Doyle wrapped his arms around him.

"Ouch, watch it," said William, removing Doyle's hand from the area on his side close to the stab wound. He looked pale and haggard. "And do try to be quiet—it's barely a quarter after six."

"Did you really come here to lecture me on the volume of my voice?"

"Of course not," said William.

"Where's Amanda?"

"She's on her way," said William. "I left in rather a big hurry. I wanted to get here. She should be right behind me."

"You drove?" asked Doyle. "In your condition? Didn't you essentially overdose yesterday, in addition to being stabbed earlier that morning?"

"Yes," admitted William. "It was a bloody fucking awful mess of a day, to be quite frank."

"Well said."

"But that's not why I'm here," said William.

"Then why are you here?" asked Doyle.

"I'm here to admit that I'm an idiot," said William.

"Well, this is quite the surprise," said Doyle. "Maybe you should come inside."

"I thought you'd never ask. I need to sit down," said William. "I have this stabbing pain in my side."

Doyle gave him a concerned look.

"That was a joke," said William, snickering.

"Hilarious," said Doyle, dryly. "You really shouldn't have driven. Amanda would have brought you here."

"I know, but she's far too cautious a driver. I wanted to get here swiftly."

"Yes, you said that. What's the rush?"

"Eva," he said.

Doyle rolled his eyes. "Listen, William, she's not the person you remember—"

"Yes, I know that now. That's what I'm trying to tell you. I'm an idiot. A drooling, helmet-wearing buffoon. I've been assuming that she's exactly the same person I married several years ago. But she's not. She's changed. I thought after two years of trying to track her down, once I found her, she'd immediately fall in love with me again. But she's not the same person she was. I'm probably not either. We're two very different people now. So much so that she wouldn't mind killing me."

"To be fair, William, she's probably tried to kill some other people, too," said Doyle, slapping William on the shoulder, which elicited a painful gasp.

"Like Wilde?" suggested William.

"You think so?" asked Doyle.

"I'm sure of it," said William.

"What makes you so sure?"

William rubbed his chin. "She's always been a very talented actress. When we lived together back in England, I was impressed with how she could go from doing an extraordinary performance at the theatre to coming home and just being . . . Eva. But since we arrived here, I haven't seen her be herself. She's always acting. I knew it, but I still . . . wanted to believe. Do you understand?"

"Oh, completely," said Doyle. "I remember when I met William Shatner. I wanted to believe so badly that he was Captain Kirk. I wanted him to say something only Captain Kirk would say. But he didn't. He just talked about his damn memoirs."

"In our teenage years, we often discover that our heroes are not who we thought they were," said William.

"No, this was last year," said Doyle. "At a convention."

Willliam shook his head.

"I brought us off topic," said Doyle. "Sorry."

Amanda walked in as William said, "It's okay."

"What's okay?" asked Amanda.

"I have rather serious issues to deal with, and Doyle is discussing Star Trek," said William.

Amanda nodded. "He does that. Should we get going?"

"That sounds like a grand idea," said William. "After all, I don't think we're accomplishing much here."

"Sorry," said Doyle. "I haven't had my coffee yet."

"Let's just go," said Amanda.

"Okay," said Doyle. "I should probably put some pants on."

"That'd be lovely," said William.

28

Only a couple hours after Doyle had decided to head to the hotel to get some rest, he was back in the car again, along with William and Amanda.

"Can we at least stop to get some coffee?" asked Doyle.

"There was a coffee maker in your room. You should have just used that," said William.

Amanda stuck out her tongue.

"Exactly," said Doyle, pointing at Amanda.

"Doyle—car!" yelled William.

"Shit," he said, swerving just enough to avoid an oncoming Scion.

"I know I've mentioned this before, but you're not a terribly good driver, are you Doyle?" asked William.

"Like I said, I haven't had any coffee," said Doyle. "And I'm sure glad you're back with us to offer up your insights."

"Absolutely," said William, grinning. "It's nice to be alive."

"I really hope Eva went to the film set. She could be heading for the Canadian border right now, completely out of our reach," said Amanda.

William nodded. "You may be right. In fact, you probably are. She's been quite the escape artist in the past. It took me a long time to find her this time. She could disappear for years."

"Then why aren't we putting the pedal to the metal and catching up with her?" asked Amanda.

"Should I?" asked Doyle.

"No," said Amanda. "Drive slowly and don't kill us."

"Okay."

William cleared his throat. "Like I was saying, we're not trying to chase Eva all the way to Canada for a couple of reasons. First, we'd be of little use trying to follow her, especially when we don't know where she's going. She could be heading down to Iowa to hide out in a cornfield for all we know," said William. "Second, we need to find out her reasons for doing what's she's done. I understand why she'd be interested in killing me."

"Here, here," said Doyle. "Not that I'd ever do such a thing, of course. But you do have a way with people, William. I think it's the constant criticisms. Or the inexplicable five o'clock shadow that never disappears."

"Thank you for that," said William, scratching his whiskers. "But my point is, I don't think we know exactly why she would kill Wilde."

"Have you told him about the bite wound?" asked Amanda.

Doyle scratched his head. "No, not yet."

"What?" asked William. "You mean the one we saw on Wilde's thigh?"

"And then I threw up on," said Doyle. "Yup, that's the one."

"The bite mark on his thigh is identical to a bite mark taken off an apple in Eva's trailer," said Amanda. "I'm sorry, William."

William nodded. "It's okay. Actually, this helps rid my mind of any doubt. She was eating an apple when I confronted her shortly after we saw the photographs."

"Well, just to add some doubt," said Doyle. "Eva wasn't in those photos. It was a wig on a mannequin head."

"Hmm," said William. "Interesting. That really looked like her."

"But still, the bite mark is fairly conclusive evidence, wouldn't you agree?" asked Amanda.

"It certainly shows a personal connection," William coughed, and continued, "or rather, a romantic connection between Wilde and Eva. I can't say I'm too terribly thrilled by that, but I suppose it is slightly better than what we thought was taking place in the photographs."

"Even if it were simply a romantic relationship, what would cause Eva to murder Wilde?"

"Maybe he was getting rough or violent with her," said William. "Or he was attempting to blackmail her afterwards, and she decided to take care of it herself."

"All things that make Eva look noble," said Amanda. "Maybe the truth is not so pleasant. She could be trying to make a name for herself. Everyone will know that *Fargo II* is the film in which Davis Wilde was shot to death. Each actor will be in the spotlight because of this, at least for a while. And remember—she called you. She wanted you here. Maybe she figured she could lead you to believe it was somebody else who did it, or perhaps she assumed the whole time that you'd figure it out, but you wouldn't let her go down."

William looked at his fingers. He tapped them together nervously. "An interesting thought," said William. "If she didn't try to murder me, then she may have been successful. Nearly dying tends to put things into perspective."

"So, what's your new perspective?" asked Doyle.

"That she's not a very nice person," said William.

The car was silent. William coughed.

"Tell you what," said Doyle. "I'm going to pull into this gas station here. We'll get some gas, some coffee, maybe a few unhealthy pastries, then we'll get to Nisswa Park bright and early, and figure some stuff out. If Eva shows up, you can have the honor of taking her down, William."

"Smashing," said William, not appearing too enthusiastic about the idea.

Amanda handed Doyle a five dollar bill.

"Here, get me some coffee, too," said Amanda. "And a scone."

"I'm pretty sure your choice is going to be a donut or a donut," said Doyle.

"I'll take a donut," she responded.

"Tea, please," said William.

"Really?" asked Doyle. "In small town America?"

William sighed. "Coffee then." He mumbled something Doyle couldn't quite make out, but sounded something like "Bloody Americans."

As Doyle pumped gas into his Stratus, a police car pulled into the gas station and parked on the opposite side of the pump Doyle was using.

When the police car's door opened, Doyle felt his heart drop. It was Officer Daniels.

I haven't even had my coffee yet, thought Doyle. *Damn.*

"Doodle!"

Doyle grimaced.

"Doodle, top of the morning to ya. You look like shit."

"Thanks," said Doyle. "It was a long night."

"Yeah?" said Daniels, trying to get a good look inside Doyle's car. "You mean, you and Merta?"

"Amanda," corrected Doyle. "But no, we were working on the case."

"Uh-huh, right," said Daniels, walking over to Doyle and elbowing him in the ribs, albeit playfully.

"So, who else you got in there?"

"That's my partner, William. He just got out of the hospital," said Doyle.

"Just got out. Right," said Daniels. "That's not what I heard, but then again, I don't really care."

"Great," said Doyle, hoping that would end the conversation.

"So . . ." said Daniels. "Looks like you got a regular Mystery Mobile right here, eh? Which one of you is the dog, and which one is the lesbian?"

"If that's a Scooby-Doo reference, it was the Mystery Machine," said Doyle. "You can be the lesbian if you want to."

Daniels squinted his eyes and stared at Doyle.

"Sorry, I haven't had my coffee yet," said Doyle.

Daniels let out a mighty guffaw and smacked Doyle in the chest with the back of his hand.

"Don't worry about it, Doodle. But don't get the coffee here. It tastes like shit. You'd be better off making coffee in your hotel room."

Doyle suddenly felt on the verge of tears. Damn caffeine withdrawal.

"What brings you here, anyways?" asked Doyle. "Didn't you say you were just going to leave it up to us to haul Eva Wong in?"

"I did say that," said Daniels. "But . . . things have gotten quite interesting."

Doyle was getting tired of hearing that.

"How so?"

"Our chief sent out a message last night directing all his subordinates to make sure the film producers have everything they need to continue filming. Our duty, so he says, is to make sure nothing bad happens on set. That's it. No searching for the psychopathic murderer. We just make sure the Hollywood phonies with lots of money are happy."

"Warms the cockles of your heart, doesn't it?" asked Doyle. "Will your chief be joining you in ensuring the safety of the rich, fake people?"

"No," said Daniels, with a look of disgust. "He's *golfing*."

"So you'll just be watching the perimeter then?" asked Doyle.

"Hell no," said Daniels. "Me and the boys already talked this morning. We want to take that Wong chick down. Some of us will be driving around lookin' for her, talkin' to other counties, try to find some leads. Don't get me wrong, I'd love it if you'd drag her in. We're just takin' the credit for it, that's all."

"Right," said Doyle. "But what about your chief's orders?"

"We'll keep things plenty secure," said Daniels. "But some of us still have some honor, y'know?" He then proceeded to spit a large quantity of tobacco juice on the concrete.

"Okay," said Doyle. "That sounds good. I'm done filling up, so I'm going to get some coffee now."

"Tastes like shit," said Daniels.

"Thanks," said Doyle, giving him a thumbs up.

29

It was barely seven o'clock, and Nisswa Park looked like the Minneapolis International Airport on Christmas Eve. Not only with the mass of people milling just beyond the front gate, but clearly whoever was in charge of the snow machine had it on overdrive. Melting slush covered every inch of ground all the way up to the busy road. *Someone spent all night on that project*, thought Doyle.

Doyle's classic, yet humble Dodge Stratus waited in a long line that also included police cars, television news vans, and plain-looking vehicles that probably belonged to the film crew members staying at nearby hotels.

"This coffee tastes like shit," Amanda said.

"That seems to be the popular opinion," said Doyle.

"Oh, God—" said Amanda.

"What? Is it decaf?" asked Doyle.

"No, not that. The security guard. That's the same guy who gave us such a tough time when we first got here?"

Doyle looked in the direction she was pointing.

"Oh, yeah. Steve the Security Guard. He was quite the character," said Doyle.

"Also not the brightest. And, oh, look, he has a gun. Fantastic," said Amanda.

Doyle eyed Amanda's coffee again. "I'm not sure about decaf, but apparently they went a little heavy on the sarcasm, Officer Hutchins."

"Give me a break. It's early," she replied.

"Fair enough. Besides, I'm pretty sure we don't need to worry about Steve. I'm certain he remembers us."

A few minutes later, they pulled up to the entrance. Doyle said, "Hi there, Steve."

The security guard focused on Doyle. Then he looked at Amanda in the passenger seat. Then he took a couple steps forward at peered in at William in the backseat. Then his eyes went wide. He pulled out his gun.

"Get out of the car," he yelled, waving the gun around.

Doyle noticed for the first time that Steve was somewhat cross-eyed. He wasn't sure if that was relevant, but he found it somewhat disconcerting to have a cross-eyed person pointing a gun at him.

"Get out of the car *now*!" Steve the Security Guard repeated.

Doyle began to open the door.

"Stop! Do *not* open that door!" screamed the guard.

"But you said—"

"Get out of the car *now*!" said the guard.

"So I should—okay, sure . . ." said Doyle, as he rolled down his window all the way, then proceeded to climb through it, and fall to the ground with a plop.

Doyle looked back over his shoulder. Neither Amanda nor William had moved an inch.

"Get out of the—" Steve was interrupted by a tap on his shoulder. The hand that held the gun jerked up in the air, causing Amanda and William to duck and Doyle to roll to the side.

An officer Doyle didn't recognize asked Steve, "What seems to be the situation?"

"Oh, hi, Frank. Did you see these three on *America's Most Wanted*?"

Officer Frank looked at the three flinching detectives. "Which episode?" he asked.

"The one last night," said Steve.

"I saw it. What story?"

"The thing in Budapest," said Steve.

Frank thought for a moment. A look of dreadful agony swept his face.

"Steve. Buddy. Are you referring to the three gentlemen that went on a murder spree in Budapest?"

"Yes! That's the one," said Steve.

"You mean the three *Chinese* gentlemen?" asked Frank.

Steve the Security Guard took another long look at the detectives. "Oh, yeah. They were Chinese, weren't they?"

Frank shook his head and turned his back to Steve.

"Then where do I know you guys from?" asked the security guard.

"We were here a couple days ago. After Wilde was murdered," said Amanda. "And in addition to not being Chinese, I'm also not a man. For the record."

Steve nodded. "Okay, yeah. That's where I recognize y'all from. I knew you looked familiar for some reason."

"I guess that's why you're the security guard, right?" said Doyle still on the ground.

"That's right. I never forget a face. Say, you can stand up now, fella," said Steve. "Sorry about that. Mr. W told me to be extra cautious today. He didn't want any hoopla or hootenanny going down today."

"I understand," said Doyle, brushing a mixture of mud and slush off his pants. "Thank God there won't be any of that."

"Damn straight," said Steve, re-holstering his gun.

"Can we go in now?" asked Doyle, getting back into his car.

"You betcha," said Steve. "Enjoy Nisswa Park."

30

"This place is absolutely packed," said Doyle. "It's like the Minnesota State Fair. Even on the off chance that Eva would dare show up today, we'd probably never see her."

"It's still our responsibility to keep an eye out for anything suspicious," said Amanda. "We just can't guarantee that Eva worked alone."

"Makes sense to me," said William, seemingly eager to shift his thoughts away from Eva for a moment.

The threesome walked through the crowd, carefully scanning everyone. Doyle noticed Officer Daniels walking parallel with them, apparently looking for suspicious activity as well. Doyle's and Daniels' eyes briefly met, then Daniels quickly turned the other direction.

"I definitely don't trust that guy," said Doyle, pointing out Daniels to the others.

"I hear ya," said Amanda. "And let's not forget about our perv with the Polaroid."

Amanda pointed to the catering table, just on the edge of the shooting area, behind the cameras. The pudgy effects man, Chip, was eating an apple danish when Doyle stepped on a twig, causing Chip to spin around and notice the three detectives staring at him. He lowered his baseball cap as if to hide and made his way to a trailer. The same trailer where only a few days ago, blanks had been replaced with real bullets, resulting in Davis Wilde's death.

"Should we go check up on him?" asked Amanda.

"Not quite yet," said William. "Look over there."

Tina, the make-up artist, was applying fake blood to Josh Hartnett's forehead. She was poking him and laughing at the same time. Clearly her flirtations were being applied just as heavily as the red goop on Hartnett's face.

"That's disgusting," said Amanda.

"I know," said Doyle. "I can't stand the sight of blood."

"No, not that," said Amanda. "It looks like she's going to jump on him right now."

"Jealous?" asked Doyle.

Amanda thought about it. "Okay, slightly. I mean, he's not bad."

Doyle could see Tina notice the detectives, but clearly didn't give them a moment's thought. She returned her attention to the handsome actor in front of her.

"Nope, I don't trust her, either," said Amanda.

Suddenly, the metal door of a trailer only yards away swung open with such velocity that the resulting metal *clang* silenced the crowd, at least long enough for Maura Coen to craft her dramatic entrance to the film set and make an announcement on her megaphone.

"*Everyone, please complete your final preparations. We begin filming in exactly twenty minutes. Again, we begin filming in twenty minutes.*"

She put down the megaphone, and the volume of the crowd swelled. Appearing as though she'd just remembered something important, she picked up the megaphone again and said, "*Once we begin filming, we will need total silence. If you're not directly working on this film and somehow made it through security, please do me a favor and fuck off. Thank you.*"

"Does that include us?" asked Doyle as loud as he could, but Maura had already retreated back into her trailer and shut the door behind her. Doyle whispered into Amanda's ear, "What do you think? Should we be fucking off?"

Amanda shook her head. "No, but Maura is yet another person I don't trust. We really have our work cut out for us here."

"Well, what do we do?" asked Doyle. "Just wander around, hoping someone tries to commit murder?"

"I think we should speak with our employer," said William, pointing at the film's producer Ronald Winthrop.

Winthrop was engaged in conversation with a man wearing what appeared to be a very abruptly thrown-together suit. One side of his white dress shirt hung loosely over his belt. His orange necktie was in sharp contrast to his black sports coat and brown pants.

"Sounds like a plan," said Doyle. "Put your game faces on."

"What does my game face look like?" asked Amanda.

"Remember when William barged in on us while we were doing the horizontal mambo in the shower? Except, you know, vertically?" asked Doyle.

"I'm supposed to look horrified?" asked Amanda.

"I was thinking angry, but you can look horrified if you want," said Doyle.

"You were also quite wet," said William.

Amanda and Doyle gave William a surprised look.

"But that's neither here nor there," said William, adjusting his collar. "Shall we get back to work? Winthrop? Yes? Very good." William took the lead, while Doyle and Amanda followed.

As the detectives approached, Winthrop and the shabbily dressed man ceased speaking.

"Mr. Winthrop?" asked William. "Could we have a moment? We have a few matters we'd like to discuss."

"Mr. Wright, it's good to see you again," said Winthrop. "And I'm certainly sorry to hear about your ex's . . . troubles."

William carefully eyed Winthrop, and turned his gaze to the man beside him.

"I really feel this discussion would best be private," said William.

"Oh, dear me," said Winthrop. "I just realize I've completely forgotten to introduce our guest. This is Chief Bernie Severson of the Brainerd Area PD—"

"That's *deputy* chief," corrected the shabby-suited man. "The chief is out playing an impromptu game of golf. He told me to get dressed and get down here, so I did—"

"That's plenty, Bernie," said Winthrop. Addressing the detectives, he said, "I assure you, any conversation can be had in front of the deputy chief of police."

William looked at Winthrop and Severson as condescendingly and judgmentally as he could muster. "Very well," he said. "Mr. Winthrop, do you really believe it a wise idea to film today? A murderer is on the loose. Everyone in this park could be in grave danger."

"Not true," said Deputy Chief Severson. "In fact, the chief told me just this morning, before he left for the Brainerd Country Club, that we're all quite safe and that filming can resume. So there you go."

"There you go," repeated Winthrop.

"Mr. Winthrop, please understand that Eva is very intelligent. She may have found a way onto the set today, even with tight security," said William.

"Unlikely," said Winthrop. "As long as the chief feels secure, I feel secure."

"But he's not even here," said William.

"Irrelevant. He'd already assessed the situation," said Winthrop.

William sighed. "Please listen to me. We think Eva Wong may have a partner. Possibly someone who's on the set as we speak. We have to investigate—"

"Okay, enough!" shouted Severson.

William abruptly stepped back, nearly tripping over an extension cord running to one of the cameras. Doyle and Amanda caught him and pulled him back upright.

"I know exactly what's going on here," said Severson. "You folks don't think us 'northerly' cops are worth a damn, is that right? We're a bunch of hicks that are too busy huntin' and fishin' to keep our town secure? We don't know what the hell we're doing, is that what you think?"

Doyle studied the deputy chief's haphazard ensemble. "Mayb—"

Before Doyle could complete his word, Amanda interrupted, "Absolutely not. We have absolute faith in the local police. Our primary concern is fulfilling our obligations to Mr. Winthrop, as stated in our contract."

Winthrop reached into his coat pocket and pulled out an envelope.

"If there's one thing I understand, it's contracts," he said. "And I also understand business. We made an agreement that you would determine who Wilde's murderer was. You managed to do exactly that. I'm sorry to see, Mr. Wright, that you've received more than your share of wounds in the process. But, I supposed that's something you're used to in your line of work?"

"On occasion," said William.

Winthrop was about to hand William the envelope when he suddenly pulled it back.

"I'll admit, Detective Wright, that I was skeptical about paying you at all for this case when I found out your ex was the culprit. It does make one wonder if the two of you weren't colluding to take advantage of me and my money. After all, you offered your services awfully quickly after Wilde was shot."

Winthrop shared a smile with Deputy Chief Severson, as if they were enjoying their own inside joke.

"But, if you were willing to take a stab wound for this small sum of money, then I suppose you deserve it," said Winthrop, finally handing William the envelope.

"Our work is nothing but honest," said William.

Winthrop smirked. "Of course."

A moment of uncomfortable silence followed.

Winthrop coughed briefly, then said, "Thank you again, detectives, for your hard work on this matter. I'm certain that Chief Severson—"

"Deputy chief," added Severson.

"Yes, Deputy Chief Severson and his crew will do a fine job of keeping our set secure while we finish the taping of our little film. I also have no doubt that the excellent men and women of Minnesota law enforcement will manage to track down and arrest Ms. Wong. Again, thank you, detectives. Have a wonderful day."

Winthrop turned his back to them and was about to walk away when Doyle yelled, "We're not done yet!"

The producer turned around and poked a finger directly into Doyle's chest. Doyle could see his face was growing increasingly red. Deputy Chief Severson held out a hand to stop him, but then pulled away.

"Yes, Detective Malloy, we *are* done. I have a multi-million dollar actor on set today," Winthrop said, pointing at Josh Hartnett, who now had an incredibly well-detailed gaping head wound painted onto his forehead. "If this nonsense takes any longer, I'm going to be out a lot of money. A lot more than your silly detective skills cost." He gestured towards the envelope in William's hand.

"But Eva Wong could have had an accomplice," said Doyle.

"I don't give a damn!" said Winthrop. "It doesn't change anything. My lead actor is still dead, and I'm still trying to piece together a shitty movie that hopefully people will still pay to see. Even if ten people were involved in Wilde's murder, it's really no longer my concern. The police can handle it. Right?"

Severson nodded and folded his arms.

"Good. Perfect," said Winthrop. "Please have these three escorted out. They're no longer allowed on set."

William simply shook his head.

"Ridiculous!" said Doyle.

"Not a good idea," said Amanda.

"Bad move," said Doyle.

"Idiotic," said Amanda.

"I love Josh Hartnett!" said Doyle.

Amanda shot a glance at Doyle.

Doyle shrugged. "I've never seen him act in person before. It might be really exciting."

Severson took a cell phone out of his coat pocket and dialed. After a moment, he said, "See where I'm standing? I want you over here right now."

"Listen," said Amanda, imploring both Severson and Winthrop. "Just leave us be. We won't interfere with the filming of your movie. And we're not charging anything more for our services. We just want to help."

Severson looked to Winthrop for his response. Winthrop shook his head.

"Sorry. You folks will have to go," said Severson. "Don't worry, though. We hicks can take care of ourselves."

31

Maura Coen stepped out of her trailer, a look of nervous apprehension on her face. She glanced down at her watch. Her eyes darted across the set, from the actors to the set pieces to the camera crew.

Lifting the megaphone, she looked into the crowd. Doyle saw her look in his direction, so he waved. Apparently she must have been looking for Winthrop, because he gave her a nod which she slowly returned.

Doyle sensed something in the air, and he wondered if William and Amanda could feel it, too. Something was going to happen. Something not good.

Maura lifted the megaphone to her mouth.

"*Bring out the wood chipper,*" she said.

"Oh, boy," Doyle said.

"What?" asked Amanda.

"Don't you remember what happened in the first *Fargo* movie?"

"No, I don't," said Amanda. "I never saw it."

If Doyle had a mouthful of water, he would have sprayed it twenty feet. "What!?" exclaimed Doyle. "How is that possible?"

"I don't know," said Amanda. "It just never happened. It's on my Netflix list, though."

"But still," said Doyle. "You're Minnesotan. It's practically a state requirement that you must see *Fargo* at least once, and then mock the exaggerated accents."

"Yeah, you betcha," said William, although his attempt at sounding Minnesotan sounded far more Austrian.

"What was that?" asked Doyle.

William coughed. "That was a Minnesota accent."

Doyle shook his head. "No. No it wasn't. Don't try that again."

"Very well," said William. "But that sounded more like you than you'd care to think."

"I don't think so, Schwarzenegger," said Doyle.

"Could you get to the point?" asked Amanda. "We may only have a few minutes before we're hauled off by Chief Orange Tie." Fortunately, Severson was looking at the activity in front of the cameras and didn't seem to hear Amanda's comment.

"Okay, so in the first movie, one of the characters chops up his fellow criminal's body with an ax and puts the severed bits through the wood chipper."

"Ew," said Amanda. "That's disgusting."

"Indeed it is," said Doyle. "Which makes me more than a little nervous about what they're about to film."

William realized where Doyle's train of thought was headed.

"You think that because one of the special effects in this film was tampered with, specifically the gunshot that killed Wilde, you believe this special effect may have been tampered with as well?"

"Exactly," said Doyle.

"That's quite disturbing," said William. "And also a frightening possibility."

"I just don't think I could live with myself if anything happened to Josh Hartnett," said Doyle. "Not on my watch."

"Well, I don't want to see your man-crush come to an abrupt end, so we should probably do something," said Amanda.

"Any ideas?" asked Doyle.

"Look over there," said William.

Two scruffy-looking men were wheeling out a giant wood chipper, followed by Chip, who was pushing it from behind.

"I'm not too keen on that Chip fellow being anywhere near that death machine," said William.

"I agree with you on that one," said Doyle.

Maura Coen once again brought the megaphone to her lips. "*Chip, get the snow machine. I want you to cover the base of the wood chipper so the base and the wheels aren't visible? Got it? Great. Everyone else, get into position. We're filming in just a moment. Where's Mike? Someone get him.*"

"Mike?" asked Amanda. "Is she talking about Mike Cameron? Is he here?"

"I don't know," said Doyle. "I haven't seen him yet."

"He was at the hospital. Did anyone ever check on him?" asked Amanda.

"Oh, shit," said Doyle. "Never occurred to me."

"I have to admit, I'm quite guilty of that myself," said William. "I was so preoccupied with recovering from a forced drug overdose and trying to locate Eva, I never once thought of how Mike Cameron was fairing."

"I imagine if Eva did something to Mike, we would have heard about it by now, right?" asked Amanda. "I mean, even though we didn't check in on him, one of the investigating officers or a nurse would have noticed by now."

"I would think so," said William.

"Where is he?" asked Doyle. "Oh, there he is."

Ronald Winthrop escorted Mike Cameron from a trailer in the distance. Winthrop was speaking into his ear. Cameron nodded as he walked.

As they stepped in front of the cameras, underneath the powerful lights, the detectives were able to get a better view of Cameron.

"He looks terrible," said Amanda. "Look how much he's sweating."

"He's probably quite nervous," said William. "Last time he was in front of a camera, he shot someone to death."

"I suppose that will stick with him for a while," said Doyle.

Winthrop gave Cameron a pat on the back and retreated from the cameras.

"Something's fishy—" Amanda began to say, when she was interrupted by someone plowing between her and Doyle.

"Excuse me, Megan. Hi, Doodle," said Officer Daniels. He tapped the back of Deputy Chief Severson's shoulder. "You called, sir?"

Severson turned around and acknowledged Daniels with a brief nod. "Yes, Daniels. I'd like you to escort these three out of the park. Can you do that?"

"Well, I suppose so . . ." said Daniels. "But are you sure that's what you want?"

Daniels leaned into Severson and said something. Doyle couldn't make out every word, but it sounded like, "They're better detectives than us."

Severson responded in his normal volume. "Doesn't matter," he said. "Everything's pretty well wrapped up at this point. The producer wants them out of the park, and we're obligated to, err—" Severson paused. "We're obligated to the people of our fair town to keep disruption to a minimum."

"Disruption?" asked Doyle, sharply. "You're the disruption here. Daniels is a disruption. This whole dang film is a disruption!"

"Where are you going with this?" asked Amanda.

"I don't know!" said Doyle. "I just don't want to get kicked out of here, so I'm becoming boisterous. Listen—Chief Severson, Officer Daniels—we don't mean to cause any harm here. We just want to help keep an eye on things. Keep people safe. That's all."

"Oh, I fully understand," said Severson. "You're suggesting we're not capable of performing our duties, is that right?"

William lifted his hand. "Pardon, Chief Severson is it? I hate to be the one to point this out, but the zipper on your trousers is all the way down, and I happen to be staring directly at your private bits."

The deputy chief's face flushed as his fingers flew to the front of his pants and zipped up in one quick motion.

"Perhaps it's best for all if you leave us be. We're very well qualified to look for even the smallest detail," said William.

Amanda and Doyle raised their eyebrows in unison. William didn't often make such pointed jabs.

Severson stared directly at Daniels, pointed to the park's exit, and said in four very distinct syllables, "Take. Them. Out. *Now.*"

Daniels put his hand on William's back and gave him a small push forward. William let out a yelp of pain.

"Stab wound," croaked William.

"Sorry," said Daniels. "Honestly, I forgot about that."

Daniels tried to shove Amanda forward as well, but she barked, "No touch."

"Fine, fine," said Daniels. "Just . . . move, all three of you. Let's just move on out of here, okay?"

"Okay," said Doyle.

They walked slowly through huddled masses of people, many of whom appeared to be from the press, or just extras waiting to be of use in the film.

"Listen, Daniels," said Doyle.

"Yeah, Doodle?"

"I just think you should know that something's about to happen," said Doyle.

"It is?" asked Daniels.

"You could feel it, couldn't you? There's just a weird sort of energy right now. Someone is about to be murdered."

"Oh, c'mon," said Daniels. "You're just trying to get me to release you guys. I'm not doing that. I have no desire to get into trouble with the chief. Or the deputy chief for that matter."

"All right," said Doyle. "But it's only fair that you should know what your superiors think of you."

"What? What do you mean?" asked Daniels.

"Well," said Doyle. "While the three of us were keeping an eye out for Eva Wong and her potential accomplice, we heard Severson and the film's producer, Ronald Winthrop, having an argument."

"You did?" asked Daniels.

We did? mouthed Amanda.

"We did," said Doyle. "The film's producer doesn't want any police or detectives around his set. Probably because he knows one of his cast members are guilty, and he doesn't want anyone being arrested. That would mean he'd have to hire a replacement and possibly re-film half the movie or who knows. You follow?"

Daniels nodded, though he continued to hustle the detectives towards the gate.

"Okay," Daniels said. "So what does this have to do with me?"

"Your boss, Chief Severson—" began Doyle.

"That's Deputy Chief Severson," said Daniels. "He's only my boss when the chief is out golfing. Which is roughly four times a week."

"All right. So Deputy Chief Severson was arguing that he wanted you to be around the set, because you're an awfully good investigator, according to him," said Doyle.

"Severson said that?" asked Daniels.

"I didn't get it, either," said Doyle. "Especially considering you wanted us to solve the crime so you could take the credit."

"Let's not bring up old stuff like that," said Daniels, punching Doyle in the shoulder.

"Fair enough," said Doyle, rubbing his shoulder. "But he does think you're a good cop. But, it does seem that your superiors, including Severson, possibly, maybe, potentially, theoretically . . . are being bribed in some way."

Doyle waited a moment to see Daniels reaction.

Officer Daniels stopped walking. "I think you might be right," he said.

"It's obvious that against Severson's better judgment, he sent you to take us out of the park," said Doyle. "The unfortunate consequence of this is that no one, including yourself, is actively watching what's happening on set. Even Severson doesn't seem to know his belt from his wristwatch, so I don't think he'll be of much help."

Daniels looked down. Finally, he shook his head. He continued towards the exit.

"Keep walking," Daniels said. "If Severson is confident enough that nothing is going to happen, then so am I."

They were just about to the gate when Amanda belted out, "He called you a pussy!"

Daniels turned around. "Excuse me?"

Amanda adjusted her collar. "Yes, your boss, Severson. He called you a . . . you know. Because he knew you'd always listen to orders, even if it meant doing something idiotic."

"Idiotic?" asked Daniels.

"Don't ask me," said Amanda. "I'm just repeating what I heard."

"You better not be bullshitting me," said Daniels.

"Trust me," said Amanda. "I never bullshit anyone. I don't even know the meaning of the word."

Daniels exhaled deeply. "Fine. Let's go back. Try to stay inconspicuous, if you can, okay? And if Severson or that producer guy notices you, it's because you snuck back in. Got it?"

"You're making a wise choice," said Doyle. "You may have saved a life."

Daniels lit up when he heard those words. "Thanks," he said. "Doodle, you know my cell. Call me if you need me."

"I will," said Doyle. "Thank you."

32

"So what's our plan of action?" asked Amanda.

"First, like Daniels said, we have to try to remain inconspicuous," said Doyle. "Otherwise, we won't do any good. So, bearing that in mind, my biggest concern is that giant fucking wood chipper. Are we all in agreement there?"

William and Amanda nodded.

"Chip," said Amanda. "We have to go find Chip. Remember, he was in charge of the bullets that ultimately went into Cameron's gun. He's probably also in charge of the wood chipper. We better make sure it wasn't tampered with like the bullets."

"Of course, if Chip has any part in this, he wouldn't tell us if the wood chipper has been tampered with or not," said William.

"We still need to talk to him," said Amanda. "Do you see him?"

"He just helped wheel out the wood chipper, but he usually seems to stick around the catering table," said Doyle.

"I see him," said William. "He's eating a corn dog."

"Let's pay him a visit," said Doyle.

The three detectives approached Chip from behind so silently and with such speed that when Chip turned around, he dropped his ketchup-covered corn dog directly onto his white Adidas shoes.

"Aw, crap," said Chip. "Hey, guys."

"Hi, Chip," said Doyle. "Let's make this quick. What's up with the wood chipper?"

"What do you mean?" he asked.

"Is it safe?" asked Doyle.

"Of course," said Chip."

"Just like the supposedly blank bullets?" asked William.

"Hey, someone switched those out. I had no way of knowing," Chip said defensively.

"Listen," said Doyle. "All we want to know is if someone could have tampered with the wood chipper. Maybe turned it from a safe set piece into a raging death machine. What do you think?"

"Nah, definitely not," said Chip. "I took the blades out yesterday. Nothing in there could do any damage."

"Where are the blades?" asked Doyle.

"In the special effects trailer, right over here," said Chip.

He led them to the trailer where just a few days before they had inspected the supply of blank bullets.

William still wasn't positive that Eva had set up Wilde's murder by herself. He knew now that she was capable of a lot of things, even trying to kill William, but breaking into a trailer seemed so . . . pedestrian. William knew she had a flair for dramatics, and Lord knew she probably enjoyed the spectacle of Wilde's face exploding on camera, but for the nitty gritty breaking and entering—she probably had help. For all he knew, it could have been Chip.

At the trailer, Chip pointed out a pad lock on the outside of the small, metal door. It was clearly in one piece.

"See," said Chip. "I took extra precautions this time. I'm not an idiot."

"Open it," said Amanda.

"Dammit," said Chip. "I was hoping you weren't going to ask that. Now I have to remember the padlock combination."

Amanda rolled her eyes.

Then, on the other side of the park, a loud, metallic, motorized whirring sound filled the air.

"That's not good," said Doyle.

"Chip, could you hurry up?" asked Amanda.

"I'm trying, I'm trying," he said. "Let's see here. Ah-ha! There we go. One, two, three."

"You were protecting the wood chipper blades with a combination of one, two, three?" asked William.

"It's the only combination I was pretty sure I wouldn't forget," said Chip.

"You still forgot it for thirty seconds," said Amanda.

"I'm not perfect," said Chip.

"William," said Amanda. "Go stop them. I don't care if we all get thrown out. That machine needs to be inspected."

William nodded. "I agree."

William was turning to leave when Doyle shouted, "William!"

"Yes, Doyle?" asked William.

"Will you grab me one of those corn dogs on the way back? They actually looked pretty good."

"They're not too bad," said Chip.

"I'm not getting anyone a corn dog," said William, and left the special effects trailer.

"Sorry," Doyle whispered to Amanda, although she wasn't even looking at him.

Amanda was glaring at Chip.

"Show us the blades," said Amanda. "Right now."

"Fine, fine," Chip said, flicking on the interior light. "They're right here."

He opened a plastic storage unit and removed a bundle of cloth.

"Are they there or not?" asked Amanda. Sweat was dripping from her brow. Doyle had never seen her so intense.

"Yeah, they're here," said Chip.

Chip removed the cloth, exposing four lengthy, jagged blades.

"Do exactly four blades go in the machine?" asked Amanda.

"Yes, four blades," said Chip. "They're all here."

"Well, that's good news," said Doyle. "Should I go tell William?"

Amanda shook her head. "Chip, where can you find more blades like these?"

Chip shrugged. "Just about every hardware store, I would think. The model we got here is one of the most popular, so any store in town oughta do it."

"Son of a bitch," said Amanda. "Where was the wood chipper last night?"

"Under a tarp," said Chip. "You know, for protection."

"You're going to need protection, you idiot," said Amanda. "Let's go, Doyle."

"Where are we going?" asked Doyle.

"To make sure that damn machine gets turned off before it hurts someone."

33

Josh Hartnett sat in his chair, reading the movie script. He knew it was his chair because a white sheet of paper with his name misspelled in crayon ("Hartnet") covered the vinyl lettering of "Wilde."

The artificial snow on the ground came up to his ankles. Even though it was made by a machine, it was still cold and wet. His socks were becoming soaked.

The gaping head wound that had been meticulously applied to his forehead by the provocative, if not somewhat off-putting make-up artist had begun to itch. He already made the mistake of scratching once, which resulted in a hand covered in fake blood. It took several scrubbings in the park's public restroom to wash it off.

When he'd heard that Davis Wilde had died in an accident on the set of *Fargo II*, he thought it would be an honorable gesture to take his place. Just like when all those actors filled in for Heath Ledger for his last movie. But so far, the experience had been miserable. Everyone working on the film was quite . . . weird.

Especially the Coen sister. Maura. She'd promised him "millions" for one or two days of shooting, even though he was only being offered a percentage of gross. He'd really only make millions if the film became bigger than *Avatar*, which Josh felt would be highly unlikely. Especially with the whackjobs working on the movie; and from what he'd read so far, a really terrible script.

Josh almost jumped five feet in the air when a horrendously loud machine was turned on. *A little forewarning would have been nice*, he thought.

Then he saw her. The director, Maura Coen. It looked like she was about to pick up the megaphone again. Time to film?

He got out of his chair and walked up to her. "Excuse me, Ms. Coen?" he asked.

"What?" she yelled over the racket of the machine.

"Ms. Coen? Are we filming soon?"

She nodded. "Yes," she yelled.

Josh opened up the script and pointed to a particular page. "Is this where we're at?" he asked.

"What?" she yelled again.

"Is this where we're at? Is my character dead?"

Maura looked at him with a confused expression. She didn't hear him.

Josh pointed at his forehead.

Then she understood. She nodded. "Yes, you're dead!"

"I don't have any speaking lines?" asked Josh.

"Huh?"

Josh pointed at his lips.

Maura shook her head. "No, you don't have any lines."

"What do I do?" asked Josh.

"Don't do anything. Just lay there!" she yelled.

"Really?" asked Josh.

"That's it," said Maura. "Go get ready. We're starting in just a couple minutes. Okay? Thank you, Josh. You look just like Davis Wilde. You know that?"

Josh couldn't hear everything, but he heard roughly every other word. "So I've been told," he said.

Josh Hartnett went back to his chair. He figured he'd better read the end. What were they planning for him?

34

William ran from the special effects trailer towards the film set as quickly as he could. He shoved people out of his way, which would normally make him feel a bit guilty, but after the gut-wrenchingly terrible week he'd had, he really didn't give a horse's bullocks.

Finally, looking towards the cameras, he spotted Maura Coen talking to the youngish actor who always looks tired.

William waved his arms in the air, as though he were stranded on an island trying to flag down an airplane. He continued to run, not letting Maura Coen leave his sights. Out of the blue something struck his windpipe, and William crashed to the ground.

William tried not to breathe because the pain was too intense. He squinted at Officer Daniels, who was rubbing the side of his hand.

"Sorry about that, fella," said Daniels. "You should really try to breathe, though."

William sucked in some air. It hurt, but having oxygen in his system was a relief.

"Now what are you doing wave your arms all over the place? You're supposed to stay inconspicuous, remember?"

"Wood chipper," croaked William, rubbing his throat.

Daniels looked at the machine that was making an excessive amount of noise.

"What about it?" asked Daniels.

"Not safe," said William.

Daniels shrugged. "As long as whoever operates it wears a pair of standard safety goggles and isn't under the influence of alcohol or drugs, then it should be just fine."

"It's for the movie," said William. He used his elbows to push himself up, but now his stab wound protested. "They're going to toss someone into the wood chipper."

"Someone? Like, a person?" asked Daniels.

"Didn't you ever see *Fargo*?" asked William, holding onto his side. He looked down to where he was feeling pain, and there was blood on his shirt. His stitches must have opened up.

"Nah, didn't see it," said Daniels. "Why?"

"Why not? It was filmed here," said William, through gritted teeth.

"I'll tell you why," said Daniels. "Because I pulled over several of those Hollywood phonies for speeding, and they were all real dillholes. So no, I won't be giving them any of my money, thank you very much."

William decided to get to the point. "In the movie, one character chops up another character and puts him through the wood chipper."

Daniels chuckled. "But that's all special effects, right? They didn't actually go and chop up a Hollywood actor."

"Well, no," said William. "But this has been different, hasn't it? One actor has already been killed. What if Josh Hartnett is murdered here in Nisswa? Do you really want all that controversy, all those people coming into your city?"

Officer Daniels didn't take long to answer. "No. No, I don't."

"Then you know what we have to do?" asked William. "We have to turn off the machine. Just long enough to inspect it."

Daniels nodded. "That's reasonable."

Doyle and Amanda showed up just as William stood, slightly swaying.

"William, why's the machine still on?" asked Doyle.

"Because of this gentleman right here," said William.

"He was making a spectacle of himself," said Daniels.

Amanda noticed the widening blood stain on William's shirt.

"Are you okay, William? Do we need to get you to the hospital?"

Doyle saw where Amanda was looking. "Jesus," he said.

"I'll be fine for now," said William. "Someone just turn off that blasted machine."

Amanda put an arm around William. All four of them headed towards the wood chipper. Deputy Chief Severson saw them coming.

"No, no, no," said Severson. "Turn right around. You're leaving. All four of you. Including you, Daniels. Turn right around."

"Listen," said Daniels. "That chipper over there—"

"Can it," said Severson. His hand hovered near his gun, although he didn't reach for it outright. "Turn around. I'm not going to ask you again."

"But you don't understand," said Doyle. "This could turn into a horrible disaster if we don't . . ."

"You're damn right this will be a disaster if you don't march your asses out of here," said Severson.

Maura Coen's voice came loudly and surprisingly clearly through the megaphone despite the noise emanating from the wood chipper.

"*Take your places,*" she said. "*We film in sixty seconds.*"

Doyle saw Josh Hartnett lay down in the wet snow, his arms askew above his head as though he'd just crashed to the ground.

Mike Cameron exited his trailer. He took a handkerchief out of his pants pocket and wiped moisture from his brow.

Doyle thought it was funny that Cameron was sweating when there was all that snow on the ground.

There was even a little snow on Cameron's nose.

Doyle stared at William. At William's neck, in particular. There was still a small, bright red mark from where a syringe had pierced the skin less than twenty-four hours ago. A syringe filled with cocaine.

"What are you staring at?" asked William.

"Oh, this isn't good," said Doyle.

Deputy Chief Severson drew his gun.

"You will move back now. Final warning," said Severson. He was sweating, too.

Amanda grabbed Doyle's hand. She looked the most nervous he'd ever seen her. She whispered into his ear. "What now?"

"This is usually where I do something really cowardly and pathetic, or something really brave and stupid," said Doyle.

"Which are you going to do?" asked Amanda.

Doyle sighed.

35

And . . . *ACTION!*

Herb Gustafson, or rather Josh Hartnett in what would surely go down as the worst role of his career, lay on the snow with a gaping head wound. Blood slowly trickled onto the white snow beside him. It spread out, diluting into a light pink, as though a child had spilled his Kool-aid.

"Ya shoulda just handed me the money, Herb," said Ken, aka Mike Cameron. "I had to go and kill ya, don't ya know."

A burlap bag with a dollar sign on the side rested at Hartnett's side. Cameron kicked it, and it flew several yards past the camera.

"I better get you into the wood chipper toot sweet," said Mike Cameron. "There's a cold front comin' in."

Cameron grabbed Hartnett by the armpits and dragged him, a trail of fake blood smearing through the snow.

"*Mike, sorry, but we have to film that over again,*" said Maura into the megaphone. "*The bag of money can't appear that light.*"

If Mike Cameron heard anything, he made no sign of it. He continued to drag the limp body of Josh Hartnett.

"*Mike, end scene. We have to re-film,*" repeated Maura.

Cameron pulled Hartnett right next to the wood chipper. Then he began to lift up.

"This won't hurt a bit," spoke Cameron into Josh Hartnett's ear.

The seemingly lifeless body of Herb Gustafson suddenly lurched forward. "That's not in the script," said Hartnett. "What's going on here?"

Mike Cameron was reaching in his pocket when Detective Doyle Malloy, specialist in celebrity cases, made his first ever major motion picture appearance. Holding the burlap sack, he ran onto the scene and tossed the sack into the wood chipper. It sprayed out in a thousand pieces, along with the goose feathers it contained. It looked like snow. Brownish snow.

"Oh, shit," Hartnett began to say, but was cut short when a blade lightly touched his throat.

Doyle saw the knife in Cameron's hand was stained with red. He wondered if William suddenly felt a phantom pain in his side.

Maura Coen couldn't see the blade from her vantage point, but she stared at the wood chipper with horror. "Ronald? Who was in charge—?" she asked, but Winthrop was nowhere to be seen. She grabbed the megaphone and directed it towards the police officers, who were watching the scene with confusion. "*This isn't in the script. He's going to kill Josh Hartnett*!"

Within moments, several guns were pointed at Mike Cameron, including those of Deputy Chief Severson and Officer Daniels. Doyle saw that Amanda was empty handed, and she was looking around wildly towards one side of the set. Doyle tried to make out what Amanda was looking at, but the lights were directly in his eyes.

"We can't let him die," said Deputy Chief Severson to Officer Daniels. "My wife loves him."

"Keep rolling film!" shouted Mike Cameron. His eyes darted around the park, as if searching for something in particular, although Doyle couldn't determine what it was. A way out, perhaps?

Doyle felt a tug on his sleeve. Amanda attempted to pull him away from the set back into the crowd, but Mike Cameron yelled, "Don't move, or I'll slit his throat!"

Doyle didn't move, although he definitely felt like soiling himself.

Not taking her eyes off Cameron, Amanda whispered into Doyle's ear, "William took my gun."

"Oh, boy," said Doyle.

"What's he waiting for?" asked Amanda.

"Probably a clear shot."

"No, not William," said Amanda. "Cameron. He's not making any moves. It seemed like he had this planned out."

"Maybe something's changed."

Mike Cameron was twitching. Doyle couldn't tell if he was extremely nervous or extremely high from the cocaine. *Possibly both*, thought Doyle. *Not a good combination.*

Doyle heard Josh Hartnett say, "Can we talk about this? I could hook you up with my agent. Maybe get you some good parts."

"Shut up, Hartnett. The only parts you'll be giving me will be coming out of the side of this machine."

The on-lookers closest to the scene groaned when they heard Cameron's comment.

"Doyle, I really don't want to see Josh Hartnett turned into haggis," said Amanda. "What should we do?"

Doyle sighed. "All right. I'll take care of it."

"What? Wait! No." Amanda tried grabbing him, but Doyle had already walked directly to Mike Cameron.

Cameron stiffened when Doyle approached, and Josh Hartnett let out a yelp.

"Whoa, let's take it easy," said Doyle. "No one wants to get hurt. I'm sure we can work this out."

"If you take one more step, I'll toss him right into this wood chipper," said Cameron. "Do you want to be responsible for that? Then get the fuck away from me!"

"Let's settle down," said Doyle. "You're not going to toss anyone into a wood chipper."

"Oh, really?" Cameron had another violent twitch, putting Josh Hartnett into a panic.

"What the hell, man! You're not helping!" blurted Hartnett.

"He's right," said Cameron. "You're not very good at this, are you? I could've been in handcuffs long before it came to this, but you were too blind."

"Hey, let's not get personal," said Doyle. "You had us fooled. You're a very talented actor."

Mike Cameron regally straightened himself and smiled. "Why, thank you. But flattery will get you nowhere."

"You didn't let me finish," said Doyle. "You're a talented actor, but you're not terribly bright."

Cameron's smile disappeared. "Is that so?"

"Shit," muttered Hartnett.

"Shit," said Amanda, shaking her head.

"Please, enlighten me, Detective. What leads you to believe that I'm not so bright?" asked Cameron.

"You could have kept us fooled. Continued to act your part. Finished the movie. Maybe we would have figured out you murdered Wilde. But then again, maybe not. You could have gotten away with murder."

"Maybe," said Cameron.

"But instead, you made your big move today. You were planning on killing Josh Hartnett. But you didn't. Instead of just tossing him in the wood chipper, you hesitated. You brought a knife to his neck. Now, you're just biding your time."

Cameron didn't look pleased.

"So what changed, Mike?" asked Doyle. "Did you have a planned escape? Did the getaway car not show up? Did Eva turn her back on you?"

Mike Cameron smirked. "I guess you have it all figured out. So what do you think I'm going to do now?"

"You have two options," said Doyle.

Mike twitched. "I'm listening."

"You can put down the knife. You'll be arrested for one murder instead of two. You'd probably serve some prison time, but you'd be out eventually."

"I don't like that option," said Cameron.

"Or . . ."

"Yes?"

"You've been threatening to murder your only chance out of here. Instead of grinding this young actor into coleslaw, use him as a hostage. Walk out of here. Steal a car. Drive off into the sunset."

Josh Hartnett's eyebrows curved into a very distinguished *WTF* expression.

"I'm not an idiot," said Cameron. "I know it's not that simple."

"It's a chance," said Doyle.

Mike Cameron looked around. He was twitching a lot now. His forehead was damp with sweat.

Doyle could tell he was nervous, but he was also considering his options.

"Fine," said Cameron, yanking Josh Hartnett directly in front of him. Mike Cameron walked backwards, using Hartnett like a shield.

As soon as he took a step behind the wood chipper, which led towards the woods and eventually the road to freedom, a shot rang out.

An audible *thump* followed.

Officer Daniels and Chief Deputy Severson immediately ran behind the wood chipper to see what had transpired.

Amanda grabbed Doyle's hand, and as they ran to catch up with Daniels and Severson, Amanda asked, "What just happened?"

"He made the wrong choice," said Doyle.

WILLIAM WRIGHT HELD THE GUN he'd used to shoot Mike Cameron. He continued to point it at Cameron as Cameron hacked up blood, due to the sizeable and likely unpleasant hole in his chest.

Deputy Chief Severson removed the gun from William's hand. "That's enough, Detective."

Josh Hartnett was lying against a tree, catching his breath. Other than a few droplets of blood on his neck, he appeared unharmed.

Officer Daniels was on the walkie, requesting paramedics.

William kneeled down next to Cameron, who was fighting consciousness. "Where's Eva?" asked William.

Doyle felt chilled by the lack of emotion William was expressing.

Cameron turned his head away, but William gently grabbed his chin and pulled. Looking directly into Cameron's unfocused eyes, William repeated, "Where's Eva?"

Mike Cameron attempted a couple chuckles before a blood bubble came out of his throat and burst.

"You still think—" Cameron began to say, but the light faded from his eyes. Neither William, nor anyone else, would get answers from him.

William stood up, but flinched from the pain in his side. He removed his glasses and rubbed his eyes.

"William—" Doyle began to say.

"Give me a minute," said William. "Please."

When the paramedics arrived, they immediately went to Josh Hartnett and removed the droplets of blood from his neck.

"Are you okay, sir? Would you like a damp towel for your forehead?" asked one of the paramedics.

As Hartnett waved them away, Amanda said, "Gentlemen . . . this man over here got it much worse."

Another paramedic saw Cameron and ran for a stretcher. Moments later, as they loaded up the body of Mike Cameron, Doyle overheard one of the paramedics whisper, "I can't believe I just saved the life of Josh Hartnett. My wife loves him."

William surveyed the crowd of gawkers.

"What's going on, William? You did the right thing, you know that, right?" said Doyle. "Listen, if you're worried about Eva, they'll catch her eventually."

"We may have been wrong about that," said William. "About her."

"What do you mean?"

"Ask around, find out if there's anyone unaccounted for," said William. "Someone was working with Cameron, and I don't think it was Eva."

"William, we've been through this . . ."

"I realize that, Doyle. But . . . the expression on his face . . ." said William. "He knew we were on the wrong track. He thought it was funny."

"What are you going to do?" asked Doyle.

"I need to search where she last disappeared. The hospital."

Deputy Chief Severson, who'd apparently overheard their conversation, put his hand on William's shoulder. His other hand was still holding William's recently fired gun.

"Detective Wright, I'm afraid I can't allow you to leave just yet," he said.

William bit back an impulsive response and instead asked, "Is there a problem, Chief?"

"You just shot and killed someone," said Severson. "I don't think the DA will charge you with anything, but this will still require a massive amount of paperwork. Needless to say, my weekend is in the shitter."

"Put me in handcuffs, bring me to jail, do whatever you need to do," said William. "*But let me do this first.*"

"He just killed the bad guy," said Doyle. "That's gotta be worth something."

Severson's contemplative expression suggested he did value what William accomplished. "I have a better idea," he said. "Let's take my car."

"Thank you," said William. "Doyle, go speak with Maura Coen. I see her just beyond that maple tree, conversing with Tina Callahan. Find out right away if she knows of anyone missing."

Doyle nodded. "Okay. Will do."

As William and Severson were about to leave, Josh Hartnett approached William and shook his hand.

"I can't tell you how thankful I am, Mister . . ." said Hartnett. Other than looking haggard from a stressful day, he appeared healthy.

"Wright. William Wright."

"William. You saved my life. I want you to know I'll never forget it."

William smiled. "You're most welcome. I very much enjoyed your work in *Milk*."

Doyle's eyed widened. He whispered into William's ear. "That was James Franco."

Josh Hartnett graciously took the awkwardness in stride. "Not a problem. I'm just happy to be here."

"Are you happy you signed on for this film?" asked Doyle.

"I'm firing my agent," said Hartnett.

"Point taken," said Doyle. He held out his hand. "It's been a pleasure for me, too."

They shook hands.

36

As William and Severson drove away in Severson's vehicle—an unmarked Lincoln Town Car—Doyle and Amanda walked directly to Maura Coen. She stopped talking mid-sentence when they approached. Tina Callahan walked away.

"Yes?" Maura asked apprehensively.

"Ms. Coen," said Doyle. "Do you know of anyone, and I mean anyone at all, who's missing today?"

"He was here this morning, but I can tell you of someone who's missing right now. Our fucking producer, Ronald Winthrop."

"Really . . ." said Doyle.

"I swear, this entire production has been one giant cluster-fuck. It's almost as if he wanted this project—my movie—to fail."

"How involved was he with the production?" asked Amanda.

"He was heavily involved after I pitched the idea to him," said Maura. "I wrote the script over a weekend in Duluth about a year ago. He was an old friend of mine at NYU, and I figured he'd have the resources to help me get this off the ground."

"I hope you don't mind me asking," said Doyle. "But what about your brothers? Joel and Ethan? I'd imagine they'd be helpful."

"We're not on speaking terms," said Maura. "Long story short, I wrote the screenplay for *Fargo.* At least the important bits of it. When the movie came out, I had zero credit. They completely snubbed me. For that, I'll never forgive them."

Doyle shrugged. "Okay, fair enough. So Winthrop liked your idea for *Fargo II*?"

"He did," said Maura. "He thought it was everything the first *Fargo* should have been. That is, had my brothers not messed with my screenplay. He immediately got to work on casting the parts, hiring the talent. He'd been attached to the business end of filmmaking for years, so he's developed far more connections than I ever had."

"He hired everyone?" asked Doyle. "Cameron, Wilde, Chip Anderson, Tina Callahan, Eva Wong . . . ?"

"Not Eva," said Maura. "She was my choice. I saw her in a low-budget Spanish zombie flick called *Dia De Los Zombies*. She was truly magnificent. Winthrop wasn't as keen on her, but I put my foot down."

"You said before that you thought Eva was guilty. Why?" asked Doyle.

"Because of those Polaroids of her watching Winthrop with Tina and Wilde. I suppose that's not conclusive evidence. She's just not a terribly social person, despite her brilliant acting ability. She can be off-putting."

Doyle nodded.

"Do you know if Winthrop carried insurance on his actors? Or crew?" asked Amanda.

Maura shook her head. "I don't believe so. Although it would have been an awfully good idea considering everything that's happened. Unless we find a way to salvage this movie, insurance would have been the only way to make any money off it. If he did buy insurance, it was without my knowledge."

"You have no idea where he is right now?" asked Amanda.

"I thought he went back to his trailer, but when I checked a couple minutes ago, no one was there. Oh, and it looks like someone stole his wigs. You might want to write up a report on that."

"Right," said Doyle. "You don't happen to know what kind of vehicle he drives, do you?

"Oh, sure," said Maura. "A red convertible Mustang. His is especially easy to spot because he has vanity plates."

"What do they say?" asked Doyle.

"RONCON," said Maura. "You know, because it's Ron's convertible."

"Of course," said Doyle.

"We should go," said Amanda.

"Right," said Doyle. "Thank you very much for your help, Ms. Coen."

"If you find Ron, tell him to get his ass back here," said Maura. "He needs to tell me how he's going to fix my movie."

"Okie dokie," said Doyle.

37

Deputy Chief Severson pulled his Lincoln Town Car into the Nisswa Hospital parking lot. William was out of the vehicle before it had a chance to stop rolling.

"Hold it there, Detective. Let's not go running off," said Severson.

"Help me search," said William. "This is where she last disappeared. She might still be here."

"That's a long shot," said Severson. "My people have already searched through this building thoroughly. I'd be quite surprised if she were anywhere in this state, let alone this hospital. I know you're hoping she's innocent, but . . ."

"I have a grand idea," said William. "Let's not speak. Instead, let's simply search the building."

"Don't have to get sore about it . . ." grumbled the deputy chief.

They walked through the front door of the hospital where just hours ago William had been recuperating from a drug overdose. William felt eternally grateful that Amanda was able to get him out in time to stop Mike Cameron from killing that young, ruggedly handsome Hollywood actor. William didn't feel good about killing Mike Cameron, but he felt less guilty since Cameron had literally stabbed him in the back.

"Excuse me, Nurse Carolyn?" said William to the woman behind the receptionist desk.

The nurse's jaw dropped when she saw William.

"Where the heck did you go? You had me worried sick!" exclaimed the nurse.

William could see from the tortured expression on Nurse Carolyn's face that she had been genuinely concerned for him.

"I'm terribly sorry," said William. "It was an emergency. Honest."

"This whole week has been an emergency," said Nurse Carolyn. "We just got a patient in here with a bullet in his chest. Deceased. Do you know how many shooting victims we get here on a monthly basis? That *aren't* hunting-related? Zero. This week? Two so far, and it's not even Friday."

"Nurse, you understand there's been a substantial amount of criminal activity taking place in the Nisswa area, yes? That's why I had to leave here early this morning. I've been investigating the murder of Davis Wilde, and now the disappearance of my ex-wife, Eva Wong."

"I heard," said the nurse. "It's terrible what she did to you."

"It wasn't her," said William. "It was Mike Cameron."

"Another one of my patients who felt he could come and go as he pleased. Except this time he came back deceased. That's why you should never leave the hospital unless you've been discharged."

"Right," said William. "I'll keep that in mind for next time."

"Sorry, I didn't mean that the way it came out," said Nurse Carolyn. "It's been a stressful week. It doesn't help that all of our equipment is on the fritz."

"What do you mean?" asked William.

"It's probably nothing," said the nurse.

"No, please . . . this could be helpful," said William.

Nurse Carolyn looked from William to Severson. The deputy chief gave her a nod of encouragement.

"I'll have Dewey show you," she said. "He's a little elderly man who helps out here once in a while.

"I've met him," said William.

Nurse Carolyn picked up a hand-held telephone and punched the "conference" button on the keypad. "Dewey to the reception desk. Dewey, please come to the reception desk. Thank you."

When Dewey, in green scrubs, arrived at reception, he was rubbing his eyes as though he had just awoken from a particularly deep sleep.

"Yes, Nurse?" he asked.

"Dewey, could you please show Detective Wright and Chief Severson what you discovered last night?"

"Oh, sure," said Dewey. "Come right this way."

Dewey led William and Severson down a familiar-looking hallway, past William and Eva's former room, then past Mike Cameron's former room, and then finally to the morgue.

As soon as Dewey opened the door to the morgue, an unpleasant odor emerged.

"What's that awful smell?" asked Severson.

Dewey looked like he wanted to say something but was holding it back. "We'll get to that," he said.

"The nurse said you noticed something strange last night," said William. "What was it?"

"Well," said Dewey. "Roughly around the same time when you had your little episode and the whole hospital went on lockdown, I came in here to lock up shop for the night. That's when I heard it."

"Heard what?" asked William.

"The motor to our refrigeration unit," said Dewey.

"You mean where the bodies are stored?" asked Severson.

"Yes, sir. It's never been a good piece of machinery. It leaks air something awful. It'll never be one of them Energy Star thingamajigs. Anyways, last night the motor was thumping something terrible."

"Thumping?" asked William.

"Yes, just a horribly loud pounding noise. I thought the whole thing was going to blow up into smithereens. So I did the only logical thing I could think of, which was to unplug the gosh-darned thing."

"Eww," said Severson. "Isn't Wilde in there?"

"Yes," said Dewey. "He's the only one. But yes, I imagine he's getting quite ripe by now. Brainerd General is supposed to be down here within the hour to pick him up, along with that new fella they brought in."

Suddenly, a loud, dull thumping sound emanated from the unit.

"See, just like that," said Dewey.

"It's not plugged in," said Severson, pointing at the electrical cord.

"Hope a 'coon didn't get in there," said Dewey.

William didn't wait to get permission. He began opening the doors to the refrigeration unit. One by one, he went down the line, growing increasingly frantic.

"Come on, come on, come on," William repeated.

When he opened the second to last door, William nearly passed out from shock and relief. Eva was inside, and she was moving. At least a little.

"My God," said Severson.

"That ain't no raccoon," said Dewey. "Why'd she crawl in there?"

"Eva? Are you okay?" asked William. He pulled out the metal slab. She was still wearing the hospital's patient robe. She moaned.

"Get the nurse," Severson said to Dewey. "Right now."

Dewey nodded. "Yes, sir. Right away."

"Can you say anything?" asked William. Eva didn't respond.

He touched her arm. It was cold. William immediately took off his clothes, everything except his underwear, and put his clothes on Eva.

"Give me your coat," said William to Severson. Severson complied. William wrapped it around Eva.

William rubbed her arms, trying to increase circulation. He didn't know how she'd survived so long. The only factors that could have kept her alive up to this point were the air leak that Dewey mentioned and Dewey unplugging the unit.

When Nurse Carolyn entered the room and realized what had happened, she immediately went to work on Eva.

"She's near hypothermia," said the nurse.

"Can you help her?" asked William.

"We treat it all winter long. But she's in rough shape. We need to get some oxygen flowing through her. *Now*. Help me get her to a room."

Dewey brought in a stretcher, and William and Severson lifted Eva onto it. Her eyes were open. William could see a faint trace of recognition in her eyes.

They rolled her to a room where Nurse Carolyn put an oxygen mask on her. She also gave Eva a series of injections, and wrapped her in a warming blanket.

"How is she responding?" asked William.

"So far, so good, but we'll see," said Nurse Carolyn. "Give me time."

38

It's gotta be Winthrop," said Doyle. He drove his Stratus as fast as he could, trying to keep up with Officer Daniels just ahead of them. Amanda kept her eyes peeled in the passenger seat. "We were right early on. It all comes down to business. He took out insurance on Wilde, and I bet dollars to donuts he took out policies on Eva, Mike Cameron, and probably Josh Hartnett. I wonder how big *that* policy must be."

"Now it seems obvious," said Amanda. "But it also seems impossible for him to get away with it. Even if he tries to collect on insurance now, he won't be able to. Not if he's brought up on charges."

"That's true," said Doyle. "I bet if he just collected on Wilde's murder, he may have gotten away with it. But he got greedy."

"Not only that, but he tried to protect himself by setting up Eva as a fall guy. It must have been Winthrop that knocked out Eva, placed her in the woods, then covered her trailer in fake blood. He wanted us to be suspicious of Eva, which of course we were."

"But once Mike and Eva were in the hospital together," said Doyle, "he figured he might get more insurance money by having Mike take out Eva."

"Hopefully he didn't succeed," said Amanda. "We'll find out if William has any luck finding Eva."

"I hope for William's sake he finds her alive. Otherwise, he's likely to have a nervous breakdown."

"Anyone would under such circumstances," said Amanda. "Doyle, car!"

Officer Daniels had whipped around a car in the right lane that was going roughly thirty miles per hour, causing Doyle to nearly smash directly into it. Doyle was able to swerve just in time. After a brief sigh of relief, he put the pedal to the metal. Officer Daniels was proving to be difficult to follow.

"I think Josh Hartnett was the straw that broke the camel's back," said Amanda.

"Is that a sexual metaphor? What're you trying to say?" asked Doyle.

"Yes, he's very attractive, but that's not what I'm getting at. Josh Hartnett was Winthrop's biggest mistake. I bet he talked Cameron into doing it, most likely promised to split the insurance money. But when he actually saw how things were going, and knew Cameron wouldn't be able to go through with the wood chipper scenario, Winthrop bolted out of there like a bat out of hell."

"How was Cameron expecting to get out of there in the first place?" asked Doyle.

"I'm sure Winthrop promised him lots of things, including an easy escape. Clearly it didn't turn out that way."

"Clearly," agreed Doyle.

Doyle's cell phone rang, with his usual "Bad Boys" ringtone. He loved the theme to "Cops."

"This is Doyle," he said.

"Doodle, it's Daniels. I just got a call from a friend of mine, an officer up in Wabedo township. He just saw our guy cruising past Woman Lake on 84. He's going to have some of his boys help us out."

"That's great news, Daniels. Thank you!"

"Anytime. Just remember, I did all the work. Right?"

"Sure," said Doyle.

"Just keep following me. We're so close, I can smell him."

Doyle snapped his cell phone shut.

"I thought of one more thing," said Amanda. "What about the photos? You know . . . Winthrop, Wilde, and Tina Callahan getting freaky, and Chip Anderson snapping the shots. What do you make of all that?"

Doyle considered this for a moment. "As you know, I've worked on celebrity cases for many years. I've noticed two things in particular that have remained consistent throughout my career. First, people in the movie industry like to have sex with each other. Second, whenever people in the movie industry are having sex with each other, someone else wants to watch."

"So you don't think there was anything devious about it?" asked Amanda.

"There certainly was. I think Maura Coen may have had every intention of blackmailing Winthrop at a later time. Once Wilde was murdered, she wanted nothing to do with the photos, and understandably so."

"Even more disturbing, Winthrop had sex with Wilde shortly before he *knew* Wilde would be murdered. That's sick," said Amanda.

"Unless he hadn't decided yet. Maybe something pushed him over the edge. But what? The bite marks?"

"Maura said Winthrop didn't like Eva from the start. Maybe he couldn't stand the thought of Wilde being with her?" suggested Amanda.

"Hopefully we can ask him ourselves," said Doyle. The "Cops" theme emanated from Doyle's pocket. He flipped open his phone and said, "Doyle here."

"Doyle. This is William. I found Eva. She's alive . . . and safe."

"That's terrific, William. Do you know what happened?"

"Mike Cameron knocked her out then shoved her in the morgue refrigerator," said William. "She was very close to death. Too close."

"You did a good job, William," said Doyle. He jumped as his phone made an exceptionally loud beep in his ear. "I'm sorry, but I have another call coming in. We'll reconnect later. You're staying with Eva at the hospital?"

"Yes, I won't leave her side," said William.

"Take care," said Doyle. "We'll talk soon."

Doyle tried his best to switch phone lines and keep his eyes on the road at the same time. He swerved across the lanes.

"Doyle, you're going to kill us. Give me the phone," she said. She grabbed it from him and hit the "answer" key. "Hello?"

"Mildred? This is Daniels. What are you two doing back there? You look like drunken Wisconsinites."

"Doyle's having issues."

"Doesn't matter. *We got him.*"

"Winthrop? Where is he?" asked Amanda.

"About five miles ahead. One of our boys pulled out and took him by surprise. Winthrop flipped his car. He's in the ditch as we speak."

"Is he alive?" asked Amanda.

"Not sure, but we'll know soon."

"Thank you, Daniels."

"No sweat, Matilda."

Within moments, they pulled up to the overturned Mustang. Smoke billowed from the engine. Four squad cars were already present. Six officers had their guns drawn and pointed towards the car. Doyle could hear the siren of an ambulance in the distance.

"Let's check this out," said Doyle.

"Be careful," said Amanda. "If he's still alive in there, he could be dangerous. I'll be right behind you."

Doyle nodded. He got out of his car and approached the Mustang, but he was immediately shoved away by Daniels. The other officers watched this exchange with curiosity.

"I'll take it from here, Doyle," said Daniels. "This guy shouldn't be too much of a threat anymore."

"Are you sure—"

"Doyle, I'm taking it from here, got it?"

Doyle didn't say anything. Then a thought occurred to him. He wondered how well the Nisswa police had conducted their interviews.

"Daniels, listen. Winthrop, he likes to—"

But Daniels didn't listen. He kneeled down near the passenger window of the Mustang. He attempted to open the door, but to no avail. The window was severely cracked, making it almost impossible to see inside the vehicle. Daniels dropped to his butt and kicked the window in.

Daniels peered inside the Mustang. Then he turned his head and looked at the other officers. He was confused.

Daniels rotated his head back to the Mustang and yelled, "Ma'am, are you the owner of this vehic—"

Before he could complete his question, a loud bang emanated from the Mustang and a bloody hole appeared in his shoulder. He fell backwards and screamed. The other officers responded with gunfire, shattering the windshield.

When a gust of wind cleared the smoke, Doyle saw the motionless body of Ronald Winthrop. His blonde wig was oozing red blood.

"I'm going to be sick," said Doyle. He thought he'd spoken to Amanda, but she was already near the Mustang, applying pressure to Daniels' gunshot wound. He ran to help.

"Bitch shot me," said Daniels, his eyes shut as he writhed in pain. "Bitch shot me."

"Doyle, give me your shirt," said Amanda.

"This is my last shirt," said Doyle. "I already wasted my other one on William's stab wound."

"Just give it to me."

Doyle did as instructed and removed his blue button-down shirt and handed it to Amanda, who immediately placed it on Daniels' bloody shoulder.

"Ow," said Daniels. "Bitch shot me."

"That was Winthrop," said Doyle. "You got him. It was all you."

"I did?"

"You took him down, Daniels," said Doyle. "We'll make sure everyone knows."

"Great," said Daniels. "Bitch shot me. Fuck this hurts."

"Don't worry," said Amanda. "An ambulance just pulled in. You'll be fine."

Daniels gritted his teeth. He opened his eyes briefly. He saw Amanda and nodded his head. Doyle imagined it was his way of saying "Thank you."

The sun was just beginning to set in the town of Nisswa, several hours after William found Eva's cold, but living body in the hospital's morgue. She'd been sleeping deeply since the nurses brought her back to a healthy temperature, and William was finally allowing himself to drift off to sleep in the chair right next to her. He'd been fighting it, not wanting to be unavailable when Eva awakened.

"William?"

His eyes popped open at the sound of her voice. "Eva?"

She was looking around the hospital room; the same one, in fact, that they'd occupied the previous evening, before Mike Cameron attempted to kill them both. Unsuccessfully.

"Did I just dream I was in a morgue? Did that really happen? Because this looks awfully familiar."

"It happened," said William. "A lot has taken place in the last twenty-four hours."

Eva was visibly trying to shake off the grogginess. Her eyes opened and closed rapidly. It looked as if she had trouble keeping them open for an extended period of time.

"You saved me. Didn't you?"

William smiled. "I did."

"What took you so long? I thought you were already dead. I'd almost given up hope," she said.

"It took me awhile to find out what Mike Cameron had done with you," said William. He felt a pang of guilt. He answered honestly, but not with the whole truth.

"Where is he now? Did you find him?"

"Yes," said William. "He's dead."

"You?"

William nodded.

Eva took hold of William's hand. Held it. "It's okay. Don't feel bad."

"I don't feel bad about that," said William. "I should have gotten to you sooner."

"You probably thought I left with him," said Eva. "Or did you even suspect Mike Cameron at all?"

William looked down. "I'm sorry, Eva."

"No, don't be," said Eva. "I don't blame you. I spent the last two years avoiding you. You were angry with me. You probably wanted me to be guilty."

William shook his head. Yet, he knew she was right.

"Still, I'm glad you rescued me. Even if you weren't entirely happy with me," said Eva.

They shared a moment of uncomfortable silence. William just wasn't sure what to say.

"You have a good partner," said Eva. "He's quite humorous. He seems genuine."

"He's a good person," said William. "Bit of a looney at times, but he manages to get the job done."

"I think you two will do well together," said Eva.

"Perhaps," said William. "I hope so."

Eva gently squeezed William's hand. "I'm going back to England," said Eva. "Soon. Once filming is complete. If there is a film anymore."

William nodded. He was disappointed, but not entirely surprised.

"Will you at least leave your number this time?" asked William. "If I need to get hold of you, I'd rather not fly halfway around the world in hopes of stumbling upon you."

Eva smiled. "Yes," she said. "But I'm hoping you'll be okay on your own. I've caused you nothing but misery since things went sour between us back home. You have a new life. A good one."

"I live in a dentist's office," said William with a smirk. "We've been paid for one case so far, and it was our first one. If I get angry at Doyle, he thinks I'm just 'being British.' My life is a mess."

"But you're enjoying it," said Eva. "You might not believe it, but I've seen you smile more times in the past two days than I saw in the last two years of our marriage."

William shrugged. "I suppose there may be some truth to that. I do like this state. The people here are so delightfully odd."

"How so?"

"A Minnesotan may absolutely loathe you, despise the very ground you walk on. But they'll still offer you something called 'hot dish.' Peculiar," said William.

Eva laughed.

Suddenly, they heard a voice yell out from a nearby room, "Bitch shot me!"

William and Eva were both silent. "That's odd," said Eva.

"That's been happening all afternoon," said William. "You've been sleeping."

"That'll be comforting to listen to."

They laughed. William released her hand and patted her on the leg. "I suppose I should let you rest up. You've been through a lot."

"Don't be silly, you've been through a lot yourself. Stay here. Get some sleep."

"But Doyle—"

"I imagine Doyle will want some time alone. With Amanda."

William raised his eyebrows. "Oh, yes. Of course. I have been walking in on them at inopportune times."

Eva chuckled. "Too bad for Doyle and Amanda."

"Too bad for *me*," said William. "I've seen things that I'll never be able to erase."

40

For you missy?" asked the rotund waitress at Rafferty's Pizzeria. It was an especially busy night. The whole town was there, eating pizza and buzzing about the events in Nisswa.

Amanda looked at the menu hungrily. "The meat lover's calzone. With extra meat."

"Excellent choice. And you?"

"The same," said Doyle.

The waitress collected the menus and walked away, leaving Doyle and Amanda to themselves.

Doyle sipped his diet Coke. "Have you enjoyed your vacation to beautiful Brainerd, Minnesota?"

"Actually, I did. Although I'd enjoy it more under different circumstances," she said.

"Such as?"

"Less murder."

Doyle nodded. "I'd suggest we head home, but I think Severson is expecting us to answer questions in the morning."

Amanda shrugged. "I can handle one more night."

From the booth adjacent to Doyle's and Amanda's, someone exclaimed, "Hartnett's suing her?"

"Yup," said another voice, "and when her brothers caught wind that she was filming a sequel to their movie, they threatened to sue her, too."

"Her own brothers?" explained the first voice.

The waitress walked by and said, "I heard she had a nervous breakdown and quit the movie. The whole kit and caboodle is bein' scrapped."

"You don't say," said the second voice. "Just goes to show ya."

Doyle looked at Amanda. "I like it when everything gets wrapped up in a pretty little package. The bad guys are dead. Eva was saved in the nick of time. The clandestine heroes are still alive to see another day."

"It's sad in a way," said Amanda.

"How so?"

"Isn't it more fun to have a cliffhanger? To be left with the feeling that great adventure awaits?"

"Well," said Doyle. "We do have a little piece of unfinished business."

"What's that?"

"William is staying at the hospital tonight. He won't be able to interrupt us."

Amanda chewed an ice cube. "You mean?"

Doyle nodded.

"Tonight?"

Doyle nodded.

"A room all to ourselves? No case to work on?"

Doyle nodded.

"Are you thinking what I'm thinking?"

Doyle nodded. "Waitress!"

About the Author

Brian Landon is a graduate of the University of Minnesota, a member of the Loft Literary Center, and the Midwest Heartless Murderers, a group of mystery writers formed under the guidance of mystery author Ellen Hart. His humorous essays have appeared in several regional publications including the Minnesota Daily, the Wake, and the Wayfarer. His first Doyle Malloy mystery, *A Grand Ol' Murder*, was nominated for the Minnesota Book Award and the Midwest Book Award. He lives with his wife, Jaclyn, in Blaine, Minnesota.

Visit Brian at
www.BrianLandon.com

ACKNOWLEDGEMENTS

Much like *A Grand Ol' Murder*, this book was a collaborative effort, a product of consistent support and advice. That being said, I owe special thanks to:

The Heartless Murderers—T.J. Roth, Jessie Chandler, and Joan Murphy Pride. I've said it before and I'll say it again . . . I couldn't have done it without you guys.

Seal and Corinne Dwyer, who took a gamble on a goofy new writer, and made a darn fine choice, if I do say so myself.

Patti Gilbert, for doing the less glamorous behind-the-scenes work. Also, for the banana bread.

Booksellers who went out of their way to promote my first book. To name a few: Janet Waller, Michele Dooley, James Orcutt, Ani Sorenson, John Campisi, and Ruta Skujins.

Readers who take the time to explore new authors, if only for the exceptionally attractive author photo on the back of the book.

My friends and family, who came out in herds to support the release of my first book. That meant the world to me.

Benjamin Rufus Landon and Clementine "C-Kat" Landon, for showing support in their own special way. Usually by licking me.

My wife, Jaclyn, who continues to be my number one fan.